F

M000096580

The Summit Murder Mystery Series

"*Murder on Everest* was an amazing ride. **Full of non-stop action and adventure**, it held my attention until the very end. Thank you authors Irion and Watkins for a great read. I'm looking forward to read what is in store for the next Summit Murder Mystery!"
—Lauren Miller, Amazon.com Reviewer

"I am a big lover of murder mysteries, and *Murder on Everest* is now on my top favorites list. **The story is unlike any I've ever read before.** Set atop one of the most dangerous mountains in the world, the elements alone are frightening, but combined with murder; it was down-right terrifying. What an amazing adventure!"
—Becky Meneely, Barnes & Noble Reviewer

"*Murder on Everest* is AMAZING…well written, great story, and **the fact that the author climbed Everest makes it even more spectacular.** Way to go and look forward to the entire series!"
—KC Summits, Amazon.com reviewer

"I couldn't wait to climb into *Murder on Elbrus* after reading *Murder on Everest*. I wasn't disappointed; the second installment in the Summit Murder Mystery Series was just as exciting as the first. **What a roller coaster ride of mystery, drama, and suspense!**
—Cindy Koelbl, Barnes & Noble Reviewer

"Once I started reading *Murder on Elrus*, I couldn't stop. The authors have developed a series unlike any other. Knowing author Charles Irion has climbed Mt. Everest and Mt. Kilimanjaro, makes the read even more exciting because he's been there himself! **The danger of the climb bled through the pages and I felt like I was there.** Well done!"
—Jake Howell, Mystery Lover

More Praise For

The Summit Murder Mystery Series

"*Murder on Mt. McKinley* is full of research and history that are weaved into the storyline, making it a **remarkable read** with an **amazing plot**. You can tell the authors did their homework. With details so vivid and writing so realistic, **I felt like I was actually there** as one of the characters on the climb right alongside them!"

—James M., Barnes & Noble Reviewer

"Mountain climbing is something very dangerous innately, when murder enters into it, it grows even rougher. *Murder on Mt. McKinley: A Summit Murder Mystery* is another entry into the Summit Murder mystery series, spinning a murder mystery around a mountain climbing expedition, focusing on each of seven major mountains around the world. **A fun read with no shortage of adventure, "*Murder on Mt. McKinley*" will prove a top pick.**"

—Midwest Book Review

"The action begins even before the ascent in *Murder on Puncak Jaya*; a Summit Murder Mystery. This thriller is action-packed and will instantly suck you in with the danger each chapter has the reader experience. An exciting read unlike any other; **the authors continue to turn out a winning series**!"

—Patricia Darnall, KOBO Reviewer

"*Murder on Aconcagua* was unbelievable! The authors made me feel as if they left me hanging off a cliff after I turned the last page! **I couldn't turn the pages fast enough,** dying to know what was going to happen next! *Murder on Vinson Massif* can't come fast enough!"

—Alan Rodriguez, Sony Reviewer

"I just closed the last page of *Murder on Aconcagua*, and WOW! What an exciting book! **The action is fast and furious and doesn't let up once** in this exciting read! Hurry up Irion and Watkins, I want more now!"

—Amber Murphy, Book Reviewer

Murder on Vinson Massif

Murder on Vinson Massif

A Summit Murder Mystery

Charles G. Irion
and
Ronald J. Watkins

www.SummitMurderMystery.com
www.IrionBooks.com

Library of Congress Control Number: 2010920776
ISBN: 9780984161867 Trade Paperback

Cover Design by Johnny Miguel, www.johnnymiguel.com
Book illustrations by Jason Crye
Book Design by The Printed Page, www.theprintedpage.com

Irion Books LLC
480-699-0068
4462 E. Horseshoe Rd.
Phoenix, Arizona 85028
email: Charles@IrionBooks.com

www.IrionBooks.com
www.SummitMurderMystery.com
www.Audible.com

Printed in the United States of America

*To the first…The American Antarctic Mountaineering
Expedition in 1966, sponsored by the American Alpine Club
and the National Geographic Society. The expedition led by
Nicholas Clinch also included the following scientists and
mountaineers—Barry Corbet, John Evans, Eiichi Fukushima,
Charles Hollister, Ph.D., William Long, Ph.D., Brian Marts,
Peter Schoening, Samuel Silverstein, M.D. and Richard Wahlstrom*

"Although we climbers usually don't admit it, we
are always more or less conscious that the strange and
irresistible call of the mountains is also a call towards
the end of life. And for that very reason we love them
all the more, and find their call more sublime. Our secret
heart's desire is that our end should be in them."
—Eldridge Rand Herron

Prologue

We'd been on our feet for 14 hours, forcing our way across the Antarctic wasteland, violent wind beating at us every step. We were exhausted—beyond exhaustion, in fact. Our mouths were parched and we'd eaten nothing for 24 hours. The storm brought with it heavy snow that struck us like icy pellets. It obscured our route and even made it difficult for us to see one another. There'd been no place for rest, no shelter of any kind since we'd set out. It was keep moving or die.

Our team leader, Esmeralda, led the way, as she had from the start. The only light in the all-encompassing darkness was the one in her hand. The rest of the climbers were cast as silhouettes against it, like shadow puppets. But despite all her strength and fortitude she was beginning to falter. Our pace had slowed appreciatively this last hour, and I didn't know how much longer she could continue.

And she wasn't alone. Exhaustion was becoming our common state. All the others were dead, but we five were still alive—we five and the killer waiting ahead of us.

I glanced at the exterior temperature on the gauge, amazed at what I saw: minus 101 degrees Fahrenheit. Was it even possible to survive in such extreme conditions? Would our space-age equipment continue to function? So far, the worst of the storm had yet to arrive. When it did—in full force—how much longer would we have?

We were cut off from all communication with the outside world. Not that it mattered. We were so isolated in the most inaccessible, deadliest, inhospitable place on earth that there was no hope of help, no possibility of rescue. We were utterly and completely on our own.

Esmeralda stopped, seeming to sway in the wind like a drunk about to totter over. A violent gust swept a wall of snow across our line, and for a moment the others appeared as ghostly figures through it.

How many were dead already? I didn't want to think about it. We'd known the risk of a winter assault on the highest mountain in Antarctica. We'd been told to trust the technology that made it possible. We'd done that—then died in droves.

Esmeralda resumed, but the climber behind her stood unmoving for a long moment. No one else stirred; then he suddenly collapsed onto the snow. I rushed over and rolled him on his back. I turned on my helmet light and reached down to open his visor.

I gasped when I gazed upon the horror before me. The man's face was hideous, a mask of sores and oozing pustules. Ominous black patches gave the appearance of a skull. He salivated from his bloated lips, and his nose streamed continuously. It was the most repugnant sight I'd ever seen.

Over the whistling of the wind he mumbled something, but I couldn't hear. How soon would we all come down with what he had, with the plague that was killing him?

I was transfixed by the ghastly specter that was lying gasping in the snow, wondering what my fate was really going to be, thinking that freezing to death might be the more merciful end for me, too.

One

Esmeralda Rickenberger looked at me as if I was crazy. Finally she spoke. "You're telling me that Raul is dead?"

Raul had worked for her, leading Andes Mountain Adventure teams to the summit of Aconcagua,[1] the highest mountain in South America, from the Argentine side of the range. "Yes. Not only Raul, but also Maria and her uncle Lucio." They'd been the film crew hired by one of the climbers to record his triumph. "They were murdered by Kira Stern." It was my first use of the word "murder," and it startled her. She bit her lower lip before speaking again.

"When did all this happen?" her voice expressing a measure of disbelief.

"Yesterday, just as we managed to escape from the mountain. Kira, helped by Carlos Oesterheld, fled to Mendoza, Argentina. I don't know where they are now. I was able to take the first plane here, to Santiago, this morning."

She tapped her fingers on the table. Esmeralda was a stunning woman. As tall as the average man, with blond hair and matching blue eyes, buxom, with glowing fair skin. We'd met for a few hours at our hotel not that long ago, just before leaving for Mendoza, at the beginning of our winter assault of Aconcagua. It seemed as though a lifetime had passed since then.

"Kira, you say? The slender Japanese woman? Isn't she a professor or something?"

1　*See Murder on Aconcagua.*

"Yes. I was as startled as you are when it first happened."

Esmeralda shook her head as if trying to find a place to fit the concept into. "There have been no reports of deaths or news about any trouble, for that matter," she said.

"I'm not surprised. But the porters are surely out by now. They will have reported what happened to the authorities."

She nodded lightly, as if that made sense. "There was a report on the local news of an incident involving the insurgents."

I sighed. I'd left that part out of my story for now. We'd climbed the mountain just three days earlier. How to keep it simple? "There was a helicopter that appeared out of the mountains, carrying insurgents from a hidden base they've got. Locals were killed in a firefight and the helicopter was destroyed." There was much more to the story but it was so incredible, I was fearful of blurting it all out. Murder and mayhem to possess three solid gold Inca idols is a tale best left to books and movies. No one was going to buy it without context, and I didn't have much time. Not if I was going to stop Kira while I still could.

"There was a report of a helicopter last summer," she said. "Anyway, Aconcagua is locked in a very powerful storm right now. There will be no word coming out of there for some days, if then. And because of the rumor about insurgents in that sector the military has heightened security in Mendoza Province—and here in Chile, as well. Something has obviously taken place."

Time to move on. "I understand you're leading this unprecedented winter assault on Vinson Massif and that Robert Ainsworth is your client."

Vinson Massif is the highest mountain in Antarctica and one of the coveted Seven Summits, each the highest mountain on one of the world's continents. Ainsworth was a very rich, elusive figure, not known to be a mountaineer until now. For reasons known only to him, he'd set out to conquer Vinson Massif in the dead of the Antarctic winter, a feat not only never accomplished previously, but never even attempted.

"That is no secret," she said, "though Señor Ainsworth asked me not to put it on our website."

Now for a bit more of the story. "You should know that Kira and Carlos are going to meet with Ainsworth. He's reportedly promised them $25 million dollars for the three gold Inca idols they have, stolen or not." There it was. Out in the open.

"Idols?" Esmeralda drew back as if she'd suddenly found herself in the presence of a lunatic.

"Kira is an archaeologist," I quickly added. "She knew the legend of the lost golden idols. There were recent rumors they'd been found, and she apparently thought there was some truth to them, at least enough to put wheels in motion. When Stern, her former husband, told her he was going on the climb she pretended to reconcile in order to join him. But, from the time we reached Punta del Inca, all she was concerned with was trying to run down these idols. Carlos operated the hostel where we stayed. He told her he could locate them—maybe she already knew that—and the two cut a deal."

Her face became immobile. "I know Carlos. I knew his father. I wouldn't call either of them dreamers."

"As I understand it, there's a lost Inca city up there, Sorojchi Huilca. According to legend, it has been buried for centuries beneath an avalanche. Inca still living in the old ways in a remote village have searched for the city and within that avalanche looking for the idols for centuries. They at last found them, and Carlos, who's lived there since he was a child, learned about it. An old man from the village agreed to steal them—for a price. Maybe somehow Kira had learned about it. In order to sound out the market for them, she'd been in touch with South American antiquities dealers who asked no questions. One of them dealt not just in stolen artifacts but also in illegal arms. He knew of Ainsworth's interest and contacted the millionaire about buying them, should he get them from Kira. The price, as I said, was $25 million. She knew about Ainsworth's climb, and once she got her hands on the idols she went straight to him, cutting out the middle man. Carlos is with her."

"She'll have to hurry. Señor Ainsworth is leaving Punta Arenas today." She gave me the kind of smile you typically see for those working with mental patients. "You must surely understand that this is all quite absurd."

"I can understand how you might think that. I'd have a hard time believing it if I hadn't lived it myself. But Kira murdered Raul, Maria and Lucio because they got in her way. She killed the old man who was selling the idols to her when it looked like he was trying to run off with them. She tried to kill me and Stern. She's desperate. She needs the money more than ever now that she's on the run and has abandoned her old life."

"You're certain that Carlos is with her?"

"Yes. They're now partners in this."

I watched her take it in. After a long moment she said, "I'm already supposed to be with the climbing team in Punta Arenas, but a family emergency kept me here. My mother was very ill. My brother, Ignacio, is running things for now. They are leaving today for Patriot Hill in Antarctica. I'm flying down later and will join the expedition there." She gave me that smile again. "There aren't many commercial flights to Punta Arenas. It is very remote."

They were interrupted then by the sound of a door opening and closing. In walked Quentin Stern, looking wild-eyed. "Is this a private party, or can anyone join?" He sauntered over to Esmeralda's desk and pulled up a chair, giving me a sideways smirk, then turned to her. "Remember me? I'm one of your customers."

"Of course, Señor Stern. I understand there was some trouble on the mountain."

"Trouble? Is that what you call it? Your guide and my camera crew were shot dead! I almost bought the farm myself. How much has he told you about what's going on?"

"He's told me that your wife is apparently the killer."

"Ex-wife," Stern snapped indignantly. "She's my ex-wife, and yes, she's the killer." He said the last with a measure of satisfaction.

"You're both certain that Raul is dead?"

"Certain?" Stern said. "He was stiff as a board when we left him. Your porters may well have dragged him behind them like a sled to get him off the mountain."

Esmeralda blanched at the all-too-vivid description, holding her hand up to stop him. "If this is true I'll have to call the authorities and his wife. She is a friend. And he leaves three children."

"We're certain," I said. "But if you'd like to wait for the porters to tell their story the authorities are sure to contact her."

She bit her lower lip. "I don't know what to do. I have to leave here in a few hours. This is an important, an historic, expedition. It's the first attempt to summit Vinson Massif in winter. I don't even know if it's possible."

"Won't it be dark down there?" Stern said.

"Yes, it is already night in Antarctica and will be for months. We'll be climbing in perpetual darkness. And it will be so cold it will make Aconcagua seem like a summer holiday."

"How is this even possible?" I asked. "Don't temperatures drop well below freezing?"

"Oh, yes. Señor Ainsworth has brought along the very latest extreme cold weather gear and equipment, specially-built shelters, snow sleds like no others, unique power sources, items that aren't for sale anywhere, some of them still experimental. Many of these things, I'm told, were designed and constructed for your military. Apparently they don't plan to fight all your wars in the desert."

"As I told you over the telephone, I've arranged for the $40,000 fee to be transferred to your bank. You may very well have it by now."

"I haven't checked." She paused then said, "I'm inclined to let you come with me, at least to Patriot Hills. But once I join Señor Ainsworth there, all the decisions are his. You'll have to persuade him to your way of thinking. Either way, you'll return with the supply plane. You understand?"

"Thank you."

"You will only have a few hours."

"What about me?" Stern demanded. "I'm coming, too."

"You have $40,000?" she asked.

He smirked again. "I've got something better. Ainsworth knows me. Trust me. The last thing he'll want is to have me go away mad. What time do we leave?"

Two

I'd done my best to ditch Stern in Mendoza. He'd been tagging along as we'd left the mountain, but I could see no value in his staying with me, just more trouble, which he attracted like flies to rancid meat. His interest was, frankly, in stopping or killing Kira. She'd told him she planned to take away their daughter, Samantha, and they were going to "vanish" with her share of the $25 million she'd get from Ainsworth for the statues. Given Stern's attachment to his daughter, that wasn't going to happen if he could stop it. In light of recent events he might settle for turning Kira over to the police, but it seemed to me he'd just as soon see her dead, one way or another. She'd played him for the sucker one time too many.

Earlier I'd called Robert Martin—if that was his real name—my contact at the Defense Intelligence Agency, or DIA, the Pentagon's version of the Central Intelligence Agency. It had been his bright idea to send me to South America with instructions to keep the Inca idols, if real, out of the hands of Hugo Chavez.

The Venezuelan president/strong man was agitating all across the continent. The insurgents along the border between Argentina and Chile were his, there was no doubt. The Russian helicopter that had nearly killed me was his, as well. And he was very tight with the new female president of Argentina, a former Red terrorist who claimed to have reformed her ways.

The statues were rumored to give the holder magical power to control destiny, foresee future events, and conquer all. The brain trust at DIA had taken the position that if Chavez got hold of them, it wouldn't much matter if any of that was true or not. Too many people in South America would figure the ball was in his court, and that would be enough for his brand of one-man, anti-Yankee rule to sweep across the continent. On top of that, Chavez was a very sick man, and those same legends claimed the magical powers extended to healing. It was heady stuff.

When I'd first heard the story I'd thought the whole thing nuts, frankly, but I was intrigued at the prospect of climbing Aconcagua in winter. I'd been there in summer, when the mountain was often climbed, but a winter climb was something else—much rarer and far more difficult.

The climb had gone as well as could be expected, with no major problems—not even from the weather. Almost all the significant difficulties had been man-made—though in this case, woman-made. Kira had been playing her own game from the first, though I'd never imagined it would descend into murder.

When I'd briefed Martin by telephone the previous night he'd instructed me to get on the morning plane to Santiago. My mission was to stop Kira and recover the idols. "This Ainsworth is untrustworthy," he'd cautioned me. "He's been tight with Chavez in the past, having sold him a wide range of military weapons unavailable elsewhere. He could very well use the idols as a means to get more business from Chavez." Ainsworth, I was told, was one of the world's leading armaments dealers.

"If Chavez can whip things up down there, Ainsworth stands to make billions. Or he might just keep the idols and use the fact that he possesses them and their so-called magic to get sales all over South America. You can't know how someone like him thinks. Regardless, we can't risk him obtaining them. We've enough trouble spots in the world to deal with without him exacerbating the situation in South America."

That the DIA would fund the expedition for me was a sign of just how serious they were, and the other proof was that they were willing to put me in the soup once again. At least, that was how I saw it.

As for Stern, getting rid of him was like shaking dog poop off your dress shoe. He'd ignored my attempts to ditch him, and I'd been distressed to find him on the single commercial flight between the two cities. Then he'd shown up at this meeting, and for some reason Esmeralda didn't seem to mind that he didn't have $40,000.

And that was very, very odd.

We didn't have any time to speak directly to each other in private because the plane was leaving that afternoon. In the taxi on my way to the airport, I sent Martin a message that I was en route to Punta Arenas with Esmeralda and Stern. He didn't answer.

At the terminal I found a quiet spot and spread out my hastily packed gear. It had served well on Aconcagua and should do the job at Patriot Hills, which was the former Chilean airstrip that was once the gateway for all Vinson Massif expeditions and a landing point for the various scientific teams that spent portions of each year in Antarctica. Patriot Hills was now largely discarded in favor of a new site, though the shelters remained in place. Martin had told me that Ainsworth had taken it over for his expedition. Though it would be very cold—well below zero, of course—I'd seen from the blogs that living conditions at Patriot Hills had been acceptable in the past, not unlike what I'd find elsewhere in a typical winter climb. However, once you moved from Patriot Hills to Base Camp, further up the mountain, it turned nasty really fast.

The single most serious problem in an Antarctic climb of Vinson Massif was the isolation of the mountain. No summit on earth was as remote. No one went near the mountain except to climb it, and there was only one expedition there at a time. In short, there was no one to call on for help.

The mountain itself was not unusually daunting, but it was high enough to present the expected problems of high altitude sickness, risk of stroke, and frostbite. Even the summer climbs were cold, and this one was taking place in the dead of winter.

And if what Esmeralda said was correct, Ainsworth was planning to make the attempt using brand new equipment. I'd served in the Army long enough to know just how unreliable that might prove to be.

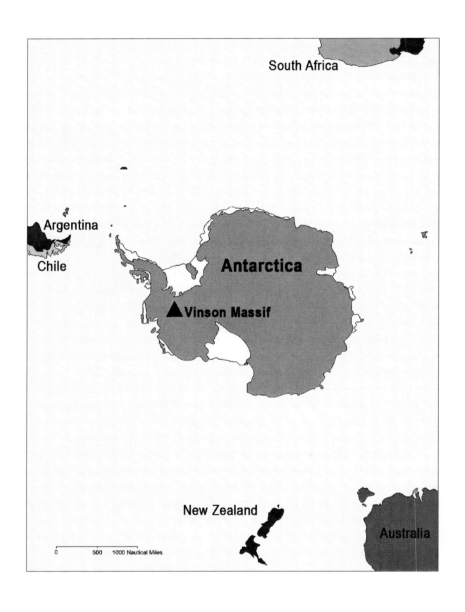

With any luck at all, however, I didn't expect to leave Patriot Hills except to return to Chile. I'd arranged to have the full fee paid only to be certain that I would get on the plane. Once Ainsworth knew Kira was a fugitive—"on the lam," as the movies say—he'd turn her over to the authorities. The websites might report that he was a ruthless international arms merchant but he was a businessman and didn't need the heat.

Or so I reasoned.

Stern arrived at the airport an hour later, dragging his gear across the floor and taking a spot next to me. "How cold do you think it's going to be?" he asked.

I'd done some research and liked nothing I'd learned so far, which was why I was determined not to leave Patriot Hills. "The mean summer temperature in Antarctica is minus 22 degrees Fahrenheit. For the winter, it's minus 76 F." These were statistics I could scarcely comprehend. And "mean" meant "average." Minus 76 was not the coldest it would be.

"It's hard to get accurate winter temperature information for the area around Vinson Massif," I continued. "When I climbed Everest[2] the temperature was minus 30 F., with strong winds adding to the cold. That was challenging. Frostbite, along with amputations of toes and fingers, you may recall, is common on Everest, and that's true even if climbers are very careful."

Having experienced Everest and other summits, I was no stranger to cold and cold weather climbs. Summit day of my summer climb of Aconcagua had occurred in the midst of a blizzard. I didn't know the temperature but would estimate it had fallen to minus 40 F in gale force winds.

But Antarctica in the winter scared the hell out of me. I could expect temperatures a full 50 degrees below the lowest I'd ever climbed in before, and under the right—or, more accurately, the wrong—conditions the temperature could plunge much lower. Antarctica was known for windy conditions that lowered the effect of already cold temperatures into very dangerous zones, the kind NASA anticipated a Mars expedition would encounter. I wasn't

---

2   *See Murder on Everest.*

even certain it was possible to climb Vinson Massif in the dead of winter, which, I had always assumed, was why no one had ever attempted it before.

"Let's just say that we don't want to be outside in these temperatures and leave it at that."

"How do you climb a mountain and not go outside? Outside what?"

"There's, like, a hotel at Patriot Hills, if you can call it that. It's series of Quonset-shaped extreme cold weather shelters that are comfortable enough. You don't want to leave them, really, Stern."

"But you have to if you want to climb the mountain, right?"

"Of course."

"So how do they plan to do it in the dead of winter if things are as bad as you say?"

"I have no idea. I don't plan on doing it."

He sniffed. "Esmeralda seems to think this can be done. She's coming."

"A good point."

"And she's got experience with teams climbing Aconcagua in winter."

"Another good point. I have no answers for you."

Stern looked at his gear. "Then I guess I'll need all this crap."

A few minutes later I asked, "What's this about knowing Ainsworth?"

Stern eyed me sideways. "We're not buddies, you understand. Tarja and Ainsworth were an item for a time."

Tarja Sodoc, widow of Derek Sodoc, had been a tabloid sensation in New York before landing the son of one of the world's richest men. She'd even dated the father, Michael, for a short time. Stern, I understood, had covered her relentlessly.[3] There was no love lost between them, as I knew.

"I take it you wrote about him."

"Oh, yeah." Stern lowered his voice. "After he dumped Tarja or she dumped him—whatever—I got to checking the guy out in detail. Get this. He bought Sodoc's Greek island, Aphrodite

---

3   See *Murder on Everest*

Ourania, from Natasha." That was Michael Sodoc's Russian wife. "You wouldn't believe the stories I could tell you about what went on there. Wall-to-wall babes, movies stars, you know? He knew how to have a good time and liked to keep it private. And there's more." He moved closer to me. "You remember how old man Sodoc died, right?"

In a helicopter explosion just outside the Everest Base Camp, I thought. Of course I remembered. I'd been standing beside Stern and we'd watched it together.

"Well, guess who sold the Nepalese air force that Russian helicopter?"

"The Russians?"

Stern smirked. "Ainsworth, through one of his companies. I wrote an investigative piece about it. I'm surprised you didn't read it."

"Investigative piece" was Stern talk for innuendo, rumor and mindless speculation, anything to punch up a story based on a foregone conclusion and story line. "You mean you suggested that Ainsworth killed Sodoc?"

"No, no, nothing like that. I just pointed out certain...facts. Yeah, facts. I can't help it if some readers formed an opinion Ainsworth didn't like. He never sued, so what does that tell you?"

It told me that maybe he liked to settle scores in other ways.

"And Esmeralda is letting you fly for free?"

"Why not? She likes good press, same as the next guy." He paused. "Not saying she's a guy, though. Did you get a look at those knockers?"

I didn't know why the lady was willing to let Stern tag along, but I doubted very seriously that good press figured high on the list. An hour later Esmeralda summoned us, and a few minutes after that we climbed aboard a chartered flight for Punta Arenas, the southernmost city of any size in the world.

The aircraft was an aged C74 Globemaster of World War Two vintage, and we sat on canvas seats along the side, staring at piled crates carefully lashed in place. The drone of the engines was such that for once Stern had nothing to say, and I soon fell asleep.

This wasn't the life I imagined after my Army discharge. I'd served in the Rangers during the Afghanistan invasion, part of one of the forward targeting teams that coordinated U.S. airstrikes with the attacks of the Northern Alliance. That was when I'd met Diana Maurasi, intrepid and perky reporter for SNS, the Sodoc News Service that comes with every basic cable package and plays relentlessly at airports. We'd started a fevered romance that, unfortunately, time and distance cooled considerably. Her work in Manhattan and mine in Massachusetts had proven too much for us. Though we'd reconnected a few times and found the magic was still there, I was convinced we had no future, despite my feelings.

After my discharge I finished my doctorate and was appointed a fellow at the Center for Middle Asian Studies. I enjoyed the work—conducting research, publishing the odd paper, participating in think tanks to project events based on traditional tribal loyalties and predispositions. The logic was that such cultures don't change all that much, and even with the trappings of the 21st century you could usually predict where such a group would land on certain issues and conflicts.

I'd done a minor project for Martin in Kabul, unaware then it was DIA I was working for. But later I realized it had been instrumental in getting me the position. Now, from time to time, he'd send me on a mission, usually to watch and report back. These promised "harmless" excursions had each turned violent, even deadly, and nearly ended in my own death. The previous month, when he'd dispatched me to Aconcagua, had been the first time I'd been given an actual mission: keep the idols, if they existed, out of the clutches of Hugo Chavez. Previously, I'd been asked only to observe and report.

Now I was finishing that assignment. The fact that Kira had murdered some very decent people, tried to kill me, and was very close to getting away with multiple murder just added to my motivation. Such were my thoughts as the plane winged its way southward. Five hours after takeoff we touched down at Punta Arenas in darkness in the midst of a violent gale.

Punta Arenas has been described a windier San Francisco, and I could see why. If there was a flat street anywhere, I never saw it, and a strong gusting wind braced me as I climbed into the hotel van. At the city center were a few multi-storied buildings, but they were the exception. The city was painted in gaudy colors, and beneath the snow covered roofs were patches of red tile.

The Hotel Cabo de Hornos was a landmark in the city center, the best hotel in the region. European-style, it lived up to its reputation. I'd never been here before but knew that Tarja had met Derek here for the first time. It was here that their fateful affair had begun. He was en route to climb Vinson Massif on his quest to climb the Seven Summits, and he'd invited her to join him. Their marriage aboard the Sultan of Brunei's yacht had quickly followed, along with an exotic honeymoon at Bora Bora. Not long thereafter, Derek was dead.

Esmeralda told us to be ready in the lobby at nine the next morning, then left Stern and me to find our separate rooms. After cleaning up and texting Martin to confirm I'd arrived, I went into the bar to see if dinner was being served. This being a Latin culture that was a silly question. The kitchen was open until midnight.

This was the off season—assuming Punta Arenas had a season—and the adjacent dining room was all but empty. The square tables were covered with white table cloths, and the male waiters were dressed like butlers. I'd hoped to find Esmeralda, as I had a number of questions for her. Instead I was joined by Stern, who plopped into the chair across from me without invitation. "I e-mailed my publishers and told them what's going on. They're pretty excited."

"They're still talking to you?" I asked.

"Why not? I've made them millions, even with that crappy lawsuit of Tarja's." Tarja Sodoc's defamation lawsuit against the publisher and Stern for what he'd written in his latest mountaineering tome, *Everest Redux*, had caused the book to be pulled from publication, though a number had already been sold. "Ainsworth is fair game. He's got no friends in the media. They all hate his guts."

"Why's that?" Just then our waiter made his appearance. I ordered Chilean sea bass, since we were in the sea bass capitol of the world. Stern ordered a bloody steak. Stern was swilling a beer. Once we were alone he leaned over and spoke in a conspiratorial voice.

"I've got a track record with this guy, and not just for the month Tarja was banging him, or him doing her—whatever. He's as bad as they come, and there's no saving his reputation. His response to anything written about him is silence. He doesn't even bother with a 'no comment.' Hell, Scott, this guy pays a publicist to keep his name *out* of print, though he can't stop everything."

"What's his track record?" I asked.

"The guy's old, maybe 50 by now. He's been at this for 20 years or more. He made his first fortune with the collapse of the Soviets. He snatched up weaponry all over Eastern Europe for peanuts, then resold it in Africa, Asia, the old Yugoslavia, Central and South America. He's got more blood on his hands than Hitler and Stalin combined. For the last ten years, he's been specializing in equipping armies and has moved up to the big time. You have to understand how this works to see where he fits in. The good old U. S. of A. sells tanks, artillery and jets to most countries. If we didn't, you could bet that the U.K., France, China, North Korea or Russia would. There's also still a really big market for Cold War small arms and ammunition. And everybody wants hand-held surface-to-air missiles. That's what this feud between Chile and Argentina is all about."

The recent dispersal of such weapons, especially shoulder mounted surface-to-air missiles, was a source of world-wide angst as nations struggled to be certain they weren't turned against commercial airliners. Such a rocket had recently brought down a Chilean air force jet. Chile was blaming Argentina, which denied any culpability. The rocket had reportedly been sold or given to Argentina by Hugo Chavez.

"He sells to Venezuela?" I asked.

Stern grinned. "Oh, yeah."

"How come you know so much?"

Stern waved his empty bottle about, looking for another beer. "I told you, I've already written about this guy, and I've had him on the back burner for a book if I can ever get rid of these mountain climbing dramas everyone wants. I'm sick of it. Cold all the time, people getting killed. Ainsworth's perfect for me. Nasty guy—and he doesn't sue." A fresh beer arrived, and Stern took a pull without acknowledging the waiter. "Right now Ainsworth is in tight with China and North Korea. He's getting his hands on some really nice stuff, the kind no Western power would ever sell to certain countries. Whatever an army—or insurgency, for that matter—needs, Ainsworth can get. This is a great chance for me to get close to him. I can probably hear enough from him to pass muster as in interview, since he never gives interviews."

"You mentioned the murders to your publisher, of course?"

"Absolutely. They love it. Fleeing murderer, intrepid reporter on the hunt, international merchant of death. Great stuff."

"And Kira? You told them the killer is your ex-wife?"

He paused. "That might have slipped my mind." He thought a moment, then brightened. "I can always use her maiden name."

"What about your daughter?"

Stern turned sheepish. "Yeah. I need to think this through, don't I?"

Just then our meal arrived. When it comes to fish, beef and wine, Chile is the most under-appreciated nation on earth. It was all perfect. Stern was content to chew for a time while I dove into the finest piece of fish I'd ever eaten. Once we slowed down on the eating he started talking again, mostly between bites—but not always.

"The real story here, you understand, is his connection to the Department of Defense."

"I thought he was black marketeer?"

"Oh, he's that, all right, but he's got a legitimate operation, as well. He manipulates the players with amazing dexterity. He needs primary access to the latest and best. There's a lot of high tech stuff being developed for the U.S. Army, and he wants a leg up in getting access for resale. He's hired a bunch of retired generals and admirals to buy influence, and he donates millions to key Congressmen."

"What kind of high tech stuff?"

"I don't know. Whatever. Desert stuff, special clothing for heat and cold, snowmobiles that operate at a 100 below zero, state-of-the-art cold weather shelters. We're going to Antarctica, and my bet is we're gonna see things made for the U.S. Army there. Count on it.

"Stern," I asked, "has it occurred to you that Ainsworth might not welcome you with open arms?"

He looked indignant. "I never said we were friends."

"Esmeralda might have a different opinion about that."

Stern shrugged. "If he understands I'm going to write about him, he'll get chummy. What else can he do? We'll be trapped down there at the bottom of the world."

My mind raced to the possibilities I was now certain Stern hadn't considered.

Three

It was just dawn at nine the next morning as I waited with Stern in the lobby. It was still windy. I understood it was always windy in Punta Arenas. Esmeralda soon joined us, not looking very happy, and the hotel van drove us to the airport.

"Just the three of us going?" Stern asked.

"Yes. The IL-76 arrived back from Patriot Hills last night and all the supplies in the Globemaster that came down with us were loaded up early this morning. It's a year-round station. They're taking and cataloging core samples. They've made some fascinating discoveries. There was some problem with the supplies they brought in last summer, and they've since developed special needs. They'll be at Patriot Hills to pick everything up. The Chilean station is located about 50 kilometers inland from there. It's closer than the new airstrip."

"Why would Chile have a research station in Antarctica?" I asked.

"Argentina has one. So do you Americans, the Russians, Japan, Finland, Uruguay and the Chinese. Something like 30 different countries. Why shouldn't we?"

I had no idea so many countries were staking a claim to the continent. "How long a flight is this?"

"Five to six hours, depending on the wind."

The Russian built Ilyushin IL-76 we were taking is a highly regarded cargo plane, expressly designed to deliver heavy loads to remote locations with less than ideal runways and in extreme weather. It loads through a rear ramp. It is a workhorse seen around the world, often used in emergency relief. There are both military and commercial versions.

There was a small area of passenger seating in front of the cargo, and there I finally managed to shake off Stern. I took a seat near Esmeralda. Once we reached altitude I turned to her and asked, "Is this climb even possible? The potential temperatures are so extreme, I just don't see it."

She nodded. "I understand. A few months ago I felt the same way, but I've been convinced it can be done. What is the expression? Oh, yes, it will be a feather in our cap to achieve this." She forced a smile. I could imagine she was burdened by the deaths on Aconcagua and concern for the aftermath. "And we're being well paid to make the attempt."

"What's the itinerary?"

"Are you planning on climbing, Señor Devlon?"

"Not me. I'm not leaving Patriot Hills. But I'm intrigued."

"You just climbed Aconcagua the traditional way, even though it's winter. You wore the standard clothing made only for colder temperatures, the same boots and gear, slept in very similar tents as you would for a summer climb. It was just a question of degree. This is entirely different, both in terms of the equipment and time. Our Vinson Massif summer climbs are scheduled for 18 days. We usually lose two or three days to weather, so typically it's three weeks. The mountain itself is not a great challenge, as I'm sure you already know. If it wasn't in Antarctica and one of the Seven Summits no one would bother with it. It's part of the Sentinel Ridge of the Elsworth Mountains on the Antarctic Peninsula. It is only 16,066 feet in height, as you Americans measure—4,897 meters for the rest of the world. The approach is in easy stages, except for the weather. You could use skis until just before the summit." She laughed.

"Yes?"

"You want to know how we're going to do it? I will tell you. We're riding high tech snow vehicles within sealed, heated compartments up to the summit until the last short distance. Only then will we get out of our bubble and walk to the top, then descend to our warm compartment. This will be a triumph of technology, Señor, not a climb."

"I suspected it was something like that."

We sat in silence for some minutes. My mind was dwelling on the pending climb, analyzing the dangers for those who would be going. Then, "You are friends with Señor Stern?"

"Not friends. We're something, but not that. He follows me around and writes books, and he blogs about these climbs and those on them."

"Yes, I do not think he has any real friends." Then she added, "And his wife did all those terrible things. Why is he going? Was she unfaithful to him?"

I could see the idea of divorce just wasn't reaching home in Catholic Chile and that while murder was seen as a problem, infidelity justified extreme measures. "I'd say so. There's a daughter at stake in this."

"The children. They are always the ones to suffer most." A male steward came out of the cockpit and asked if we wanted coffee or tea. We both took coffee. "You met Carlos Oesterheld at the hotel in Punta del Inca?"

"Yes."

"I wasn't surprised to hear he is with Señora Stern in this, not if there is a lot of money to be made."

"Why is that?"

"His father was a Nazi. Did you not know that?"

"No." I remembered what Stern had told me the first time he'd seen Esmeralda. In his mind, everyone in this part of the world of German extraction was a Nazi.

"This is a well-known story in Punta del Inca, where I first heard it. His name was Joachim Oesterheld. He was in the SS, part of a special commando, a team that retrieved artifacts from all over the world. Hitler and Himmler, head of the SS, were fascinated by the occult. You saw that movie *Indiana Jones*? It is based on these people. This Joachim had Himmler's confidence. Anyway, during

the Second World War Himmler heard about the Inca idols. Yes, they are an old story. Joachim was sent to find them if he could. There were many Germans in Argentina willing to help. He soon identified the region about Aconcagua and settled in to search properly, but by then the war was going against Germany. By the time it ended he'd still not found the lost city where the idols were said to be. Given his history, he had no choice but to stay on when the war ended. He lived in Mendoza for a time, but then the war crimes trials started and he moved to Punta del Inca and built the hostel. I don't know what he did in Europe that he was nervous about, but it was something very bad, I think. He spent the rest of his life looking for those idols."

"And Carlos?"

"He is a Nazis too, Señor. Argentina still has them. Not many, but some. But those who remain are very dedicated and carry on the work. Carlos, he is one of the worst, and in his case, he has very good reasons for hiding out in the mountains."

"So you're saying a chance to make a fortune is something he'd jump at even if a few people had to die?"

"Oh, yes. He's is not unfamiliar with death." She paused as if about to say more, then seemed to change her mind. "He has searched for those idols all his life, just as did his father. You tell me they found them, they have them. He will do anything now, anything at all." Then she added, "Obviously, he already has."

We lapsed into silence. I nodded off for a time come awake as the plane descended and banked for landing. I looked out the window and could see the vast expanse of snow and ice below, lit only by the stars. The sky was a deep ebony, a stark contrast to the leadened expanse below. It was a strange, surrealistic vision, unlike any I'd ever seen before. In the distance I made out the sharp blue lights outlining the runway, the area to each side oddly dark and unoccupied. A short distance away was a cluster of glowing objects I took to be the base itself. It all looked forlorn and lost amid the vast expanse of night and the endless sea of snow.

We touched down more lightly than many commercial liners, taxied a short distance, then came to a stop. Outside, flashlights pierced the darkness, and there was movement forward as a ladder was extended from the side of the plane with a thump.

"Dress warm," Esmeralda said as she stood up. "It is about to get very, very cold."

And was she ever right. As the door opened I stepped from the plane and an icy embrace enveloped me. It was the coldest cold I'd ever experienced, made worse by a strong breeze sweeping across Patriot Hills from the Antarctic interior.

I spotted two Snowcats off to the side, each hitched to a train of empty sleds. There were some odd-looking loaders, as well, unlike anything I'd seen before. Perhaps 200 feet away were the large, glowing tents I'd spotted from above that made up the camp here. Directed by one of the mummy-wrapped men brandishing a flashlight, I didn't need to be prompted twice. I set out toward them as quickly as I could, following Esmeralda, who went straight to one of the structures.

Once through an exterior door I found myself in a dead zone. When Stern closed the door to the outside Esmeralda opened the one into the interior and filed in. We quickly followed. The shelter was a long "barrel" which was nicely appointed, considering its remote location. This end was a gathering place, with a number of chairs scattered about before small tables. Standing beside a radio set was a familiar looking man dressed in boots, insulated trousers, and a heavy, woolen shirt. He looked to us, then turned back to the seated radio operator. Just beyond them were two large dining tables, joined end-to-end. Beyond them, separated by a plastic wall, was a kitchen.

A handsome man came over and spoke quietly to Esmeralda in Spanish. She nodded, then introduced Stern and me to her brother, Ignacio. The Spanish heritage was stronger in him than her, but he had the size and build of a German. "A surprise to see you, but a pleasure," he said as he shook our hands.

The seasonal use of this location had recently ended with the relocation of the expeditions to Union Glacier. There they could take advantage of a naturally occurring runway atop a frozen blue ice lake. It was now closed for the Antarctic winter.

The man I'd first seen patted the radio operator on the back, then approached me with a smile. "Captain Devlon," he said, using my Army rank at separation. He had strong features and heavy lips. His physique and woolen shirt projected the image of a lumberjack. "You might remember me from our short stay at KK in Uzbek, and later in Kabul." KK was the Karshi-Khanabad military base in Uzbekistan.

There'd been five Ranger teams in all. We'd been flown to the dilapidated former Russian barracks for orientation as manpower and equipment were brought in. Twelve days after the start of the air assault on the Taliban then controlling Afghanistan the Ranger teams had been inserted and, following an early contact with the enemy, thereafter had operated independently. Red Team, which I'd led, had been at the point of the assault and received the most publicity, but we'd all stuck our necks out and done our part. I recalled that this was a man with whom you did not want to bet on a pool game when highly intoxicated. The more intoxicated he became the steadier his hands.

"Of course. Tusk…something."

He grinned. "Bryan Tusker, just Bryan these days. It's good to see you. I hope we can catch up." The smile faded. "I don't understand why you're here, though. You're not listed as part of the climbing team."

"I need to see Mr. Ainsworth on a matter of great urgency. I was able to persuade Esmeralda to let me fly in."

He nodded lightly. "He's with someone right now in his shelter. I'll let him know you're here and what you want. If you don't see him sooner, chow's at six."

"I take it you have some other unexpected visitors."

"A couple and another man, yes. You'll see them, too. Right now we need to get you settled. The earliest you can return is tomorrow, when the IL does its turn around. We'll be busy until then. The scientists from the Chilean Research Station are here and eager to get the bird off loaded; one of them is very sick and needs to get to a hospital. Well, I don't know how Mr. Ainsworth is going to take your presence, but you've got at least one friend here who is happy to see you."

Stern raised his chin and spoke. "I'm Quentin Stern, the journalist. When can I interview Ainsworth?"

Bryan lifted an eyebrow. "Have you already arranged that? It's not on the schedule."

"I've come some distance at considerable expense. I'm sure he'll want to meet with me."

"I'm not his secretary. I'll let him know you're here, but he's a very busy man right now. The expedition sets out tomorrow."

"Still…"

Ignacio had been in a corner, conferring with his sister. Bryan glanced their way as he cut Stern off. "I'll take you two to your quarters now. The plane takes off after breakfast, which is at eight. You should be prepared to be on it. No one will be here except a couple of my men to keep the camp operational. Everyone else will be on the first stage of the expedition, which, as I say, leaves tomorrow, as well."

Outside wasn't bracing, it was just plain cold. The breeze had picked up, if anything, and during the short walk to our shelter I was quickly frozen to the bone. I counted eleven of these Quonset-shaped shelters, set in two rows. Snow was banked three feet up each side. Again we passed through a double-door system before entering a brightly lit, long barracks. There was a small group of men gathered around a card table. There were a dozen narrow beds spaced evenly from there along each side. At the far end I could see someone sleeping. Ignacio pointed us to empty beds and told us our gear would arrive shortly.

Bryan waited for me to strip down to indoor clothing, then suggested we have a sit. He lifted a bottle of brandy from a shelf with one hand while taking two glasses with the other. He looked at me with arched brows. "Sure." I sat next to him as he poured two and handed me a glass. He glanced at Stern, who, for once, had the sense to stick to his own business.

"I don't know how much you know about what's going on here," Bryan said in a low voice, "but I thought I'd take a few minutes and fill you in."

"I appreciate it."

"Ainsworth reopened this camp last month expressly for this expedition. He's flown in enormous quantities of supplies and special equipment. Except for you two and the three who flew over with him, everyone here works for the man. He's not a mountain climber. He's a fitness nut, you understand, but no outdoorsman. He's tackling this mountain in the dead of winter because it's never been done before and because he wants to impress the U. S. military chain of command as well as burnish his public image a bit.

"But there's more to it than that. I can't go into it, but use your head and you'll get it. In several of these heated shelters is some of the most sophisticated cold-weather gear and equipment ever designed and built. Many pieces of it are prototypes. Ainsworth got it directly from the DOD vendors. These shelters here are standard issue for Antarctica, double sided, durable. The ones to be used on the expedition though are another thing entirely. So are the ETVs—Extreme Temperature Vehicles—the climbers will use. Very special, no real metal except where essential, and then special composites designed for intense cold.

"He's also got these suits we'll be using; they look like space suits to me. White, flexible joints, a round helmet with a clear visor. You could wear these things on Mars, which, I understand, is where the basic design and requirements came from. They started out as NASA projects before the military stepped in."

"He's testing all this, then?"

Bryan nodded. "He's got an inside track to sell under the radar. If this stuff works as intended he stands to make a killing, you understand?"

"Why would the Army want anything like this?"

"Russia is pretty cold, I hear, so is northern China, Mongolia, North Korea and the north slope of Alaska, for that matter. And then," he gestured slightly but took in the vast expanse around us, "there's all this for the taking. Right now this is supposed to be international territory, but it's rich in resources. A number of countries have staked out claims already. The long-range planners, I'm told, think the day may come when resources are depleted, when it will all be up for grabs."

He emptied his glass, took a refill, then topped mine without asking. "Let me tell you the players. Ainsworth's got his girlfriend with him. You'll likely see her. Former model named Rhea Harsten. Nice lady with a drug problem."

"She's climbing the mountain?"

He laughed. "Not hardly. I think she's along to cut her off from her supply. They've got a complicated relationship. She'll wait here for the hero's return. As I say, you're going back after breakfast, so you may not see her at all. He's got a security guy with him, a Cuban, Angel Pagan, like the ballplayer. But this guy's no angel, he's all pagan. Stay away from him. I'm in charge of the gear, and I've got eight people with me. They're all ex-military, and some aren't so 'ex,' if you follow me. You'll have no trouble spotting them."

"What are you doing here?" I asked.

"Now, that's a story in itself. The short answer is, I'm making a lot of money." He finished his drink and stood up. When he spoke, it was directed at Stern and me both. "You were already in the dining shelter. Dinner is at six, like I said. Don't wait for an invitation." With that he left us to settle in. As promised, our gear arrived a few minutes later.

Four

Stern, two others in our shelter, and I reached the dining shelter just before six. Nothing outside had changed, and I was frozen through and through by the time we were inside. I'd forgotten I'd skipped lunch until the first ripe aroma reached me.

The man, as Bryan had called him, was standing just inside the entrance as we ducked in. He eyed Stern and me carefully as we stripped off our heavy coats and headgear. Behind him at the table were Kira and Carlos, seated across from each other. Carlos was looking the other way, while Kira had eyes only for Stern—and not in a good way. It made me wonder just who was stalking whom.

And there was Evaristo Zapata, sitting on the other table, closer to us. He spotted me and flashed a slight, almost apologetic, smile. Most of the other seats at this end were taken up with staff from the looks of them—fit, rugged looking individuals—and four bearded men in different clothing, bookish, with pale skin and speaking Spanish. I took them to be scientists from the Chilean research station.

Bryan approached Ainsworth and spoke quietly to him. He nodded approval of some kind, then went to the head of the tables and took his place between Kira and Carlos. Bryan gestured for Stern and me to sit at the far end, next to the scientists.

My hunger was gnawing a hole in my side, and by the time I was served it was all I could do not to wolf the food down. Ainsworth

was content to eat and exchange pleasantries with Kira, who had turned on her engaging persona. Carlos finally looked my way, and for the first time I really grasped what Esmeralda meant when she'd called him a Nazi. At Punta del Inca he'd just been the friendly hotelier, but his look now revealed the dead eyes of a killer.

Just then a wave of cold air enveloped us and in came a tall, slender woman. Once she'd removed her thick, fur-lined coat and tossed her hair back I was struck with her great beauty. This would be the former model, as out of place here as a summer rose. She looked at Ainsworth, a look that turned into a glare when she spotted Kira laughing beside him. He glanced up, then said something to Carlos on his left. Carlos got up and moved down to a seat nearly opposite Zapata. The murmur of conversation resumed as the model moved to the now open spot and sat down, flashing Ainsworth a brief smile before giving Kira the "drop dead" look of one female competitor to another.

I wasn't alone in being hungry and, fortunately, there was plenty of food. Bottles of red Chilean wine sat on the tables and were soon replaced by more. There was an understandable level of tension in the air. The scientists were disheartened, but apparently both Esmeralda and Ignacio apparently knew them well and soon had them smiling. Carlos ignored us, while Kira continued to engage Ainsworth in conversation, the other woman having lapsed into silence as she picked at her meal.

When dinner finished, Bryan came to me. "He'll see you two in his shelter. I'll take you over in a few minutes."

Ainsworth gave me a brief nod of recognition as he put on his heavy gear and was joined by the model, Rhea. He was, I noticed, four inches shorter than she. I guess a lot of men who date super models get used to that.

Kira and Carlos remained seated some distance away. Zapata had joined the scientists in conversation, speaking mostly to one in particular. There was no love lost between him and the other two. He was here for the same reason I was: to get the idols away from them. In his case, however, he planned to turn them over to Hugo Chavez, who would then use them to spread revolution and chaos throughout South America. I understood he'd been shot fleeing Punta del Inca, but I saw no sign of a wound.

Ten minutes later Stern and I were in Ainsworth's private shelter. It was, of course, more spacious than the others and comfortably appointed. It was divided into rooms, and there was another barrier to keep the cold out of what I could only call the living room. There was also a large, expensive throw rug covering most of this area, the only such rug, I imagined, on the entire continent.

He rose when we entered and shook my hand. "Good to meet you." He was looking at me, so I assumed he didn't include Stern in his pleasantry. "Please have a seat. I trust dinner was satisfactory. Can I get you something? I've no servant but have no objection to seeing to you myself."

"No, thank you," I said. "I'm comfortable."

"I'll take a Coke," Stern said.

"A Coke?" Ainsworth appeared startled at the request for a moment, then said, "Would you care for a splash of Bourbon with it?"

"No. A Coke's just fine."

After giving Stern his drink Ainsworth sat in an overstuffed mauve loveseat facing us where we had taken seats beside each other on a couch. The furniture could not have been more incongruous. "What can I do for you two?"

I put his height at five feet nine inches. He was buff man, muscled with the kind of conditioning you get from gyms. His bright, even, well-tended teeth nearly glowed in contrast to his tanned face. He was losing his hair and cropped what was left almost to the scalp. His eyes were strikingly dark, approaching black. They were impenetrable, yet piercing. He was clearly in charge and accustomed to staying that way. There was more to him, though, an aspect I couldn't quite put my finger on, as if he were somehow poised on a personal precipice.

"Let's start there, Mr. Ainsworth. Stern is not with me. There was just the one flight from Mendoza to Santiago, and he was on it. He persuaded Esmeralda to let him come on today's flight here from Punta Arenas. You'll have to ask her why. I'm here to speak to you about something that has nothing do with him and is, candidly, none of his business."

Ainsworth nodded, staring at me curiously. "And you?" he said to Stern.

"I've come to stop my wife, Kira." Stern went back and forth on this. Now she was his wife. "She's threatening to take my daughter away from me."

"You've flown to the Antarctic over a domestic dispute?"

"No, no. You see, we were in Argentina together, climbing Aconcagua. She killed our guide, Raul. He worked for Esmeralda. Then she killed my film crew, Lucio and Maria. She even tried to kill me!"

Ainsworth smiled with bemusement. "I've heard of no killings associated with the mountain." A tick started in the corner of his left eye.

"It all just happened, and it's in a remote area," Stern continued. "It might be a few days before news gets out. But it will!"

"Perhaps. She said you'd accuse her of terrible things, that there'd been some deaths. Of course, mountaineering is a dangerous undertaking, especially a mountain such as Aconcagua in wintertime. I don't know if either of you have stayed in touch with the situation, but that entire region is on military alert. There's a report of a helicopter attacking a military outpost."

"No, no, no. It attacked us!" Stern said. Then he smirked. "You should have seen it crash."

"Crash?"

"Yeah, we shot it down."

"A helicopter attacked a group of mountain climbers and you shot it down. That's what you're saying?" He looked at me in disbelief.

"Exactly," Stern said smugly.

"I wasn't aware that mountaineers carried guns on Aconcagua." He lifted his hand and rubbed at the tick.

"I...I guess they do," Stern stammered. "At least some of them did this time."

"I remember you," Ainsworth said forcefully, as if suddenly recalling something. "You wrote those very unpleasant stories about me."

"Not me! That was my editor. They take a fair story then they punch it up and run it with my byline. They like to hide behind the reporter. I never had it in for you."

Ainsworth pursed his lips. "You've gone to a lot of trouble to find me," he snapped. "What is it you want?"

"I want you to arrest Kira and send her back to Chile to face the music!" Stern hesitated. "And since I'm here, I was thinking you might give me an interview."

Ainsworth smiled. "I'm not a police officer. If she's done anything wrong—and she says she has not—that is a matter for the authorities. I'm here to climb a mountain, my first significant one. It will be an historic event." At that he glanced my way. "I've invested a great deal of money in this enterprise, as you can see, and I'm on a very tight schedule. My meteorologists have informed me we have a rare window of less frigid than usual conditions with little wind. I can't let anything interrupt me. I'm sure you understand."

"Let me…"

"That will be all, Mr. Stern. You can find your way back to your shelter. Plan to be on the morning flight."

Such was Ainsworth's presence that, for once, Stern shut up. He climbed into his gear and left the two of us alone. Ainsworth regarded me for a long moment with those black eyes, then asked, "A drink? I'm having Jack."

I smiled. "In that case, I'll join you."

Once he'd settled back into his comfortable chair he said, "I've read about you, but as you can tell, I have little confidence in what I read about anyone. Look at the lies that have been written about me." He glanced at the exit. "Many of them by that man. What can I do for you?" He flashed a smile which vanished so quickly it was unsettling.

"I want the idols." I'd decided to put it bluntly. He struck me as a man who liked straight talk, or at least understood it. "I'm here to get them."

Ainsworth smiled. "They aren't mine to give."

"Kira and Carlos aren't going to give them to me. I don't see them doing much if you just take them."

"I can't either—but I'm not a thief. And I have no reason to take them."

"But they've been offered to you to buy."

"Ye-es. I'm undecided. And they want a lot of money."

"Kira really is a murderer. It *will* come out. If you harbor her here, it will go against you."

"You're assuming those killings, if true, will ever come out. An enormous storm has struck that region, as I said. You were lucky to get out when you did. No one is going in for some time, and when they do, who knows what they'll find. And if this report of a helicopter attack is true, any killing will be attributed to it, I would think. Argentina has a lot on its plate with Chile right now. I can't see it being in their interest to pursue killers who are long gone. And they'd have to say something about the idols, wouldn't they? That could be very awkward. Better to hush the whole thing up. That's my reading."

"You're saying Kira and Carlos are going to get away with this?"

"I'm saying it's not as clear cut as you might think. And it's true, I'd like to have those idols. Did you see them up close?" I shook my head. His eyes lit up and he leaned forward. "Terrible beauties. There is something powerful in them. And the eyes. They burn right through you. I couldn't help but wonder how many deaths they've witnessed. You can see why some people might think the legend about them is true." He moved back on the seat. "But the woman wants, as I say, a great deal of money."

"Have you talked to Zapata?"

He didn't answer other than with a delicate shrug of the shoulders. Ainsworth was close to Chavez. It seemed to me it was in his interest to deal with Zapata. Of course, Zapata didn't have the idols, either. And if he did get them, they'd end up with Chavez or Castro, not Ainsworth. Still, they were here—in Kira's backpack, for all I knew. This didn't have to be difficult for Ainsworth if he didn't want it to be.

"Why do you care about the idols?" he asked. Again he rubbed at the tick.

Now, that was a very good question and one I'd posed to Martin, knowing it would come. I'd been given an answer. "I'm representing a U.S. government agency in this matter. I can't prove it, so you'll have to take my word. The idols are considered a matter of national security. The reasons should be self-evident. You'll make some friends in Washington with your co-operation."

Ainsworth smiled at that. "I've had my problems with the Department of Defense, and I can always use friends there. I work for high stakes in a very competitive profession. Lies and disinformation are as much a part of my world as is influence peddling." He shook his head sadly. "It's the way of the world, unfortunately. I'm testing this equipment for DOD vendors in the most extreme conditions and at great personal expense—and some risk, I might add. There are those who will be very appreciative when Bryan's team delivers its report. My situation will be improved for a time." He took a sip of Bourbon. "But since I don't know *who* you represent, I can't put much stock in what you say. I know you for climbing mountains."

"What I'm saying is true. Turn the idols over, see me on my way, and I'll report it. It really should be of help to you."

Ainsworth paused, then shook his head lightly. "Not when you consider the other friends I've got, and the new ones I'm making, with this expedition. Refill?" I had another drink. Ainsworth took a long pull once he'd settled in, then changed the subject. "When you reach a certain point in life you begin looking for new challenges. I've followed your career very closely, for example."

"You mean the books and so-called documentaries."

"Yes. Keep that in mind when you consider my own media coverage. Everyone blames those who supply weapons for what happens, never those who use them. Still, you seem intent on climbing the Seven Summits. I forget. Did you make it to the top of Elbrus in Russia?"

"No, the minister died before we'd gone very far."

"Maybe next time, then. But you've knocked off Everest, twice I think, Mt. McKinley, Puncak Jaya and Aconcagua, twice, as I understand it."

"You're right. You have been keeping track."

Ainsworth smiled. "I've even read that man's books." By "that man" he meant Stern. "I want you to know that I never believed you had anything to do with Derek Sodoc's death, despite his insinuations."

"He cleared that up in his second book."

"I've read it, too. But there were three documentaries, by my account, that presented your actions in less than favorable circumstances. I'd like to hear the story from you."

"It was a long time ago."

"Not so long, and when will I get another chance to learn the details firsthand? You may not know that I bought Derek's yacht, Windsong. I always admired him enormously. I have copies of every one of his televisions shows and specials. Not with me, of course."

"I heard you bought his father's Greek island, as well."

"I did. It is magnificent. I don't know if the stories told about it are true or not. I can only hope. And I've enjoyed myself there immensely." He laughed. "I've turned day-to-day operation of it over to a Greek university. They're slowly restoring the vegetation and wildlife to pre-civilization levels. The village there will serve as a center for ecological studies that, it is hoped, will make a re-forestation of Greece possible. The land has been brutally mistreated by man for millennia."

Robert Ainsworth—philanthropist. That was a new twist. I wondered what dirty deal was in it for him.

"Tell me about Derek," he asked. If I wanted the idols I really had no choice. So I did.

I wasn't Derek Sodoc's best or oldest friend. I'd first met him when I'd traveled to Argentina to climb Aconcagua the first time. We'd run into each other at the Hotel Ayelen in Penitentes, and he'd invited me to join him at his table in the bar. We were on the same expedition. That climb had been struck with a brutal storm that created winter-like conditions on summit day. Another friend and

I had all but carried Derek back down, saving his life. Three people froze to death that day, their bodies never recovered. Derek had insisted I join him a few months later when he tackled Everest, and I'd agreed. Every subsequent event had flowed from that decision.

Only son of one of the richest men in the world, ruggedly handsome, fit, an international playboy and celebrity with his own television show, heir to his father's vast world-wide media empire, I'd found Derek a bit overwhelming at times. He'd refused his father's path, elected to carve out his own career, but daddy wouldn't leave him alone and Derek hadn't the strength to resist him in total.

The consequence was that his every exploit received maximum media attention and, tragically, his bid to climb the Seven Summits became a media sensation, ending in his death at the Hillary Step, not far below the summit of Everest. It was to be the culmination of his quest; instead, his body remained frozen there for a year until his father paid for an expedition to recover and return it.

"Was he really murdered?" Ainsworth asked when I stopped.

"Yes. He was alive when I left him, but he was killed not long after."

"Amazing. Simply amazing. And you saw his father blown up in the helicopter?"

"Yes, he'd just threatened to have me killed before stepping into it. Stern was standing beside me."

"Why would he want to kill you?"

"He was killing everyone associated with the climb on which Derek died. He blamed us all. He refused to face the fact that he'd pushed his son to his own death by causing him to take a reckless chance."

"Very interesting. We must talk more about this. I'm fascinated." He glanced at his expensive wristwatch. "But, unfortunately, not tonight." He took a sip of his drink, then asked, "What do you think about this climb of mine? I value your opinion."

"I don't see how it's possible. So-called 'summer' is tough enough here; winter is unimaginable"

"Normally I'd agree with you. Dressing for cold weather in standard gear, hiking in the dark and extreme cold, setting up the camps with the customary tents, I agree that it can't be done that way. As I'm sure you know, I'm no mountain climber, but I've long been intrigued at the thought of scaling tall mountains." He laughed at the humor of the situation. "I've often wondered what Derek would think of my plan. I can just picture him here with us, eager to take on the challenge. Ever considered Vinson Massif?"

"No. Too cold. And that's in the summer."

"Don't you know it. It's a bitch in summer, and this is dead winter. It's been dark for two months, and night will continue for months more. But I was telling the truth earlier. We aren't getting warm weather, but we are getting summer-like conditions for the next week. That means, at worst, temperatures of about 70 below, 20 degrees warmer than typical." He saw my look. "You haven't seen the equipment yet. It's in shelters, being kept warm. It's designed to withstand 100 degrees below zero, I'm told, though I don't intend to find out. Want to know how I'm going to do it?"

"Sure."

"It's pretty simple. We're leaving tomorrow morning—not that morning here means much without the sun. The summer climbs Esmeralda leads take up to three weeks. She uses a Base Camp, then two camps from there. Three in all. You have to acclimate, of course, so certain delays are built in. I'm taking Diamox to speed the process. I've cut out all the dawdling and plan to do the assault in seven days. I could actually do it in less with the gear I've got, but as you know, the human body only builds its cell count so fast, even with help."

"And you've got your seven days."

He flashed that unsettling smile. "I never expected that. You can see why I don't need all this." He waved his hand lightly, as if dismissing the distraction of the idols.

"Send everyone home. I'm prepared to take my chances with the police in Punta Arenas. Once the Chilean government has the idols, that's as good as my getting them as far as I'm concerned. I'll leave it to my government to deal with them."

He eyed me steadily then said quietly, "But you forget, I haven't decided yet if I'm going to buy them."

His girlfriend came out from the rear just then, looking very comfortable in some scarlet fleecy night thing that reminded me of a bunny outfit. It certainly revealed why she'd been a model. She seemed to have forgiven Ainsworth his conversation with Kira.

"Who's your friend?" she murmured as she sat beside him, lacing his feet with hers as she took his hand. He introduced us.

"We're discussing the climb. Scott here's an expert. I'm hoping to persuade him to join me. He was also a good friend of Derek's, and that will give us time to talk about him some more."

"Were you? That will make you very popular here. Are you going to join Robert?" She spoke in an airy voice and looked at me through sleepy eyes usually reserved for the bedroom.

"I don't think so," I said.

"I'm still hoping to persuade him." Ainsworth finished his drink. "Kira and Carlos are coming, you know. When I told them I had gear for them they became quite enthusiastic."

"You believe that?

He smiled. "I believe they want something from me. I told them what I'm telling you: this climb has all my attention. I won't be making any decision about those idols until *after* I summit. I have no time for distractions. You understand?" I nodded, and he continued, "Consider my offer overnight. You can give me an answer in the morning. I doubt we'll set out any sooner than noon. Things will be in turmoil until the plane takes off and the scientists are gone. The climb will only take a few days the way I've got it worked out, and I need those days to give what you want real consideration. You can't expect an answer from me on the spur of the moment, can you?"

"I've not come prepared for a climb in these conditions. I've got only the gear I used on Aconcagua."

He scoffed at the idea. "I've got plenty. We have redundant snow vehicles and the new arctic extreme suits. They are all really something. You don't want to miss a chance to see how this is done." He leaned forward with enthusiasm. "This will be one for the record books, I can tell you."

"It still sounds very cold."

"And dangerous," Rhea said. "I'm worried for Robert. If he wants you to come, you really should."

"Nothing to worry about, honey. And not so dangerous," Ainsworth corrected. "Not if you do it right. I've got it all covered."

"And all the equipment works like it's supposed to?" I added. "It rarely does on first use, you know."

"There is that, isn't there. I really appreciate your talking to me about Derek. For the first time I feel as though I understand him. He's a very sympathetic person, don't you think?"

"I liked Derek. He didn't deserve what happened to him."

"No, he didn't." Ainsworth stood up. Time to go. "Think about it. The way I've got this set up, this climb should be a snap for you. I'd really like you to come. And you'll have plenty of time to convert me to your way of thinking." With that he grinned and turned back to his beauty.

Five

Laughter was coming from the glowing dining shelter as I approached. I ducked in to warm up before going on to my own. The scientists had cast off their gloom and were taking advantage of the free booze and female company. Esmeralda was enjoying herself, as was her brother standing beside her.

Stern was out of sight, but Zapata came up to me with a drink in his hand and a contemptuous look on his face. "I'm surprised to see you here," he said. He was a slender man, six feet tall, with a trim mustache and thick glasses. His dense, dark hair was white at the edges. I'd once thought that he possessed a scholarly look, but I'd since seen him in action and knew that for the façade it was.

Zapata had joined our Aconcagua expedition in Mendoza. My DIA control had told me that he was a skilled operative for both Cuban and Venezuelan intelligence. His current mission was to acquire the idols for Chavez, or, in the alternative, for Castro. With the idols, either man would be in a position to cause great harm and turmoil in South America, not to speak of the many lives that would be lost.

"I'm sure we can co-operate while we are here."

"You shot Fowl, remember? He'll live, by the way. Thanks for asking." Lester Fowl, an aging CIA cold-warrior, had also been on the Aconcagua climb and told me that his objective had been Zapata. Just what that objective was remained vague in the telling.

As near as I could determine, he was to recruit him if possible, keep him away from the idols if they actually existed, and…What? Kill him? I never knew.

Regardless, after the murders Zapata had been our temporary ally in the search for Kira, Carlos and the idols. We'd cooperated in the pursuit, been shot at, had one of our party killed, and then, when Kira was in sight and we in a position to seize her and the idols, he'd turned on Fowl and shot him.

"I never thought the wound to be serious," Zapata said dismissively. "I had no choice, since he was determined to stop me. Surely you knew that. He is a CIA spy, after all. I know all about him. If I'd wanted him dead he'd be dead, I assure you."

"You betrayed him and me." In both the military and on climbs, betrayal was the worst offense a man could commit.

Zapata glared for a moment, then said, "I was shot, as well." Stern had snapped off several rounds at the fleeing Zapata after he'd tried to kill Fowl. I didn't believe for a moment that wasn't Zapata's intention.

"Not seriously, I take it."

He touched his side. "It is most painful. I would say that Señor Fowl and I are even."

"I'm pretty certain he holds a different opinion." I wasn't up to making small talk with Zapata. It was just a bit too genteel for my stomach. I walked off without another word.

Esmeralda was refilling her glass. "Ainsworth has asked me to join the expedition," I told her.

"You've paid for it," she answered neutrally.

"That was just to get me here."

She reflected a moment, then said, "So he's going to buy those idols."

The scientists laughed at a joke. When they quieted, I said, "He said he's thinking about it."

"Señora Stern, his wife and Carlos are also coming on the climb." She gave me that poker face look again.

"So I understand." I watched her finish her drink. "Is that a good thing?"

"It isn't my decision," she answered.

"I can't imagine you want to be on a climb with Carlos."

"I've climbed with many people I don't like. I run a business."

"When you talked about him earlier I sensed there was more to the story than having a Nazi for a father."

Esmeralda shrugged. "His history is well known in certain circles, if you are interested." I nodded. "You know about Argentina's so-called Dirty War?"

In the late 1970s and into the early '80s, the generals ran Argentina. The so-called "war" was against its own people, and upwards of 30,000 disappeared and another 15,000 were imprisoned. Something similar had happened in Chile in 1973 when the generals killed the president and took power. General Augusto Pinochet subsequently ran the *junta* that ruled for more than a decade. Some 2,000 were killed, another 25,000 arrested and subjected to various degrees of torture. By the late'80 s, democracy had taken root again. In both countries, dealing with the military murderers had been, and remained, problematic, as a part of the deal for stepping down the generals had demanded amnesty. The result was that many mass murderers remained unpunished and at large.

"I've read the modern histories of Argentina and of Chile."

"Then you know. My older brother, Bruno, did not like Pinochet, so he went to Buenos Aires to attend university. He was studying to be an engineer. Then the same thing happened there. He thought he could stay out of it, since he was Chilean, but they took him anyway. The generals didn't care that he was from Chile. In their eyes, he was a communist."

"I'm sorry to hear that. You must have still been a child when all this happened."

"Yes. A toddler, as you Americans say. I adored my big brother. He was like a father to me. He was a half-brother, you understand. My father's first wife died giving Bruno life. Let me tell you what they did. You would be kidnapped off the street by men in civilian clothes. If your family or friends went to the police, they were told that there was no record of such an arrest, that he must have been the victim of a criminal kidnapping. As far as the authorities were concerned, it was as if Bruno never existed. No record was kept of these abductions. Everything was word of mouth—spoken, never written. Their jailers would take the detainees to a cell where they would beat and torture them until they learned all they knew. Even if they knew nothing, by the end they would make things up just to stop it. Reports have been published. You should read the terrible things these people did." I thought for a moment that she might cry.

"But the worst part was to come, because they did not release them." Any thought of tears had vanished replaced now with hatred and a lust for revenge. "What they did instead was set them free. You wonder how that was? I will tell you. They would go into your cell and give you a shot which would make you very drowsy. Once you were easy to handle they would load you, along with other detainees, also 'pacified,' into an airplane that would fly out over the South Atlantic. The door would be opened and one by one they'd push all of you out the door, setting you free three miles up. That is what Carlos did to my Bruno."

In my shelter I shucked off my heavy coat and prepared for bed. Stern was already sprawled across the bed beside mine, still fully clothed, though without boots. "Get the idols?" he asked.

"No. He's still considering buying them. I don't think he and I are on the same page."

Stern grunted, then said, "I was talking to one of these support guys about what's been going on." I sat on my bed and gave him my full attention. "They think it's nuts spending all this money to climb the mountain in winter."

"I agree. What about the equipment? Ainsworth expresses a lot of confidence in it."

"Some of these guys tested it, which is why they're here. We've got prototypes here, you understand—these aren't production models. Their concern is reliability, but they said they've been subjected to arctic conditions and will work. The one guy said that if they didn't have to stop for acclimating, they could get there and back inside of five days. They don't like Ainsworth much. They think he's a little crazy."

"Why are they here?"

He leaned over and lowered his voice. "What I heard was that some of these guys are still military assigned here on temporary duty. The Army doesn't want this stuff out of its control, though they don't mind learning how it does in these extreme conditions, especially since Ainsworth is picking up the tab for everything. The other guys are ex-military, and—get this—they're getting paid $200,000 each. I told you this guy is rolling in dough."

"What about Kira?"

"What about her? She and Carlos tried to sell him the stuff, and like you said, he's thinking about it, which infuriates Kira and Carlos. They're also getting really nervous. They want to be long gone, not climbing a mountain. Anyway, I heard that Ainsworth spent a lot of time on the sat phone after meeting with them. He's nervous about buying the idols. What really pisses me off is I wrote an article about Ainsworth a couple years ago and named one of the middlemen he uses in South America. Guess who Kira went to after talking to me and learning I was coming on the Aconcagua climb? She's been hitching a ride with me the whole way."

"Where are the idols?"

Stern gave me a greedy look. Gold has that effect. "That's a good question. Kira might have hidden them in Puenta Arenas, you know. If she brought them here she'd be risking having them stolen. If that happened, what would she do? She's got no one to go to."

"How can she sell them if she can't show them to him? He already told us he saw them. Remember?"

"Maybe that was in Chile. But I'd say they're here somewhere. She may need to give him another taste, and she needs them at hand to turn them over if she seals the deal. I'll bet she's got them in their stuff. You plan to steal them?" He sounded excited at the possibility. "She's pretty sneaky, you know. They'll be well hidden."

"I'll take them if I can. But I don't see that happening. I'm going back tomorrow."

"He didn't want you to go on the climb?"

"What makes you ask that?"

Stern leaned up on his elbow. "Because everybody does. People drop dead like flies around you on these climbs, but you're the famous Scott Devlon and everybody wants to take you along. It's like Russian Roulette, if you ask me. It's a game some people just can't resist. And Kira's going, you know. You won't want her out of your sight. You've got to dog her until you've got the idols."

At times, Stern could be quite perceptive. I sighed with sudden realization. "Where are Kira and Carlos sleeping?"

He shook his head. "Beats me. In one of the other shelters. They don't want us to know." He sniffed. "Did you hear about the sick scientist?" I shook my head. "The guy who analyzes their ice core samples came down with some strange disease. They're flying him out of here, but he's so sick that they aren't sure he'll make it. I guess Ainsworth was enraged when he learned of it. He's afraid they've exposed everybody to a new communicable disease."

"Have they?"

"Esmeralda says they don't know anything about it but have no reason to think it's connected with the samples they've been bringing up. But you have to wonder just what stuff's been frozen down there for thousands of years, maybe foreign ancient unknown bugs we've got no immunity to."

"I think I've seen that movie, more than one of them. Next you'll be saying we'll be turning into aliens and drinking human blood."

Stern looked at me sharply. "I'm not saying that. I'm just asking, what if he's caught something from the past? If we keep fooling around with these things we know nothing about, the day will come when something's going to bite us in the ass. We think we know everything, but the truth is, we know next to nothing. And this outfit isn't exactly open about what it's up to."

"What's that supposed to mean?" Stern was notorious for his conspiracy theories.

"You can find it on the Internet. I read a blog that says the Chilean Research Station started out as a legitimate project. Two years ago the military took it over. The story goes they found something down there."

"Found something?"

"Some bug, I think. Chile isn't exactly a world power, but a strange bug from the past, something we don't have immunity to, would make a powerful military weapon."

"I don't think Chile is out to rule the world."

"I'm not saying that. Just listen. This blogger says the Cubans are involved, even the Venezuelans. They're looking to get a refined version of this bug. Now one of the scientists is sick? Put two and two together."

"A blog, you say."

"So?" He looked at me indignantly then coughed lightly. "I think I'm coming down with something."

Because we existed in perpetual night so close to the South Pole, morning was no colder than the night before. Only a change in weather pattern, which generally meant wind, influenced the temperature. I'd slept in surprising comfort and had been able to have a hot shower before dressing for breakfast. Stern was gone when I'd arisen, and he wasn't in the dining room when I entered.

I found it warm and noisy. The flight crew was with us this morning. I'd not seen them the previous night. The scientists looked hung over, and I doubted they'd slept much. Esmeralda was with her brother, the two apparently discussing the day's events. It was going to be a busy one for them. The scientists would set off with their supplies for their camp while Stern and I returned to Punta Arenas with the plane. I really couldn't see Carlos and Kira going on the climb, despite what Stern and Ainsworth had said, so they'd likely be with us. Ainsworth had his mind set on this climb, and we were all just a distraction to him. Plus, there were other buyers.

Still, I had to acknowledge the unmistakable glow in his eyes when he described seeing the nasty little things. Gold, idols, and their legends have a way of causing even the powerful and shrewd to do things they'd normally never consider.

Breakfast was generous, the coffee excellent, and the company robust. I've rarely enjoyed myself more. As the scientists left to get ready to set out, I joined Esmeralda and Ignacio in going outside and watching. The two Snowcats I'd seen on arriving were theirs. They were already running and had, I now noted, sealed cabs. Connected to them were four sled-mounted trailers each. The men waved jauntily as they came out of their shelter carrying their personal effects, then dividing themselves into the Snowcats. With headlights piercing the darkness and the trains lit with yellow and red lights, the procession set out amid the roar of engines. We waved goodbye then ducked back in.

"I'm surprised to see them with Snowcats," I said inside. "Are they reliable here in winter?"

"They are at these temperatures," Ignacio said. "They're really for the summer, but these are summer-like conditions right now. The problem arises when you encounter really cold weather. Normally they'd be down for the long winter and wouldn't use the cats at all, but there was a problem with their last shipment of supplies, so they risked it. They got lucky with the temperature. They're a good bunch. I see them down here two or three times a year."

It was hard to believe that he and Esmeralda were brother and sister. She looked as if she'd just come down from the Bavarian Alps, while he resembled a Spanish hidalgo. She was a large woman, full-figured without being in the least fat, while he was tall and trim. He spoke with a slightly heavier Spanish accent than she did.

I drew another cup of coffee and took a seat at the far end of the two tables. Kira and Carlos were here now, looking very tense. There were, as well, several of the support staff. They were fit men, quiet, with a distinct military look about them. Zapata was sitting with them, and the flight crew had located themselves between us, staking out neutral territory. Esmeralda and her brother spoke in Spanish, still planning the morning preparations, as the expedition was setting out in a bit.

After a few minutes the door opened and in stepped Bryan. He motioned for me to join him. I went over, and he told me that "the man" wanted to see me. I donned my outside clothing and followed him to Ainsworth's shelter.

Inside was a swarthy, stout man with an acne-scarred face who gave me the once over from where he stood. I took him to be Angel Pagan. I'd wondered when he'd turn up.

Ainsworth was sitting on his couch, holding a coffee mug with both hands. He was dressed in bright clothes much resembling ski attire. Bryan moved a respectful distance away, so it was just the two of us.

"I trust you had a good night's sleep?" he asked. I told him I had. "We worked hard at the amenities here. I also hope you gave my invitation consideration?" I shrugged lightly. He finished his coffee, then set the mug down.

"The expedition sets out in a few hours. I have the opportunity to make history. You've seen the extent of the operation here, and you believe you have an idea of the expense involved. I assure you that you are not even close. This is important to me, now that I've committed to accomplishing it. Failure is out of the question. That's one reason why I want you to come. You will bring a great measure of expertise to this endeavor.

"I've considered your story and am prepared to accept that you represent whom you say you do. But you must understand my position. Yesterday Kira and Carlos arrived in Punta Arenas at the last minute with an incredible story and, yes, with the idols. Zapata had his own version of events. I neither believed nor disbelieved them. Then you also arrived, with Stern, Kira's former husband. You two told an equally incredible story. It is impossible to confirm what anyone is telling me because of weather conditions around Aconcagua and because of the heightened military alerts in Chile and Argentina. Weather also dictates what I must do here, which is leave at once.

"As for these idols, some weeks ago a dealer I know contacted me to say Kira had a lead on them. She'd offered to sell them to me if she could locate them, and she quoted a ridiculously high price. You must understand that I get contacts like this all the time. In fact, I received an anonymous contact two months ago about these same idols, which was the only reason I was willing to give Kira's query any credibility at all—that and her professional credentials."

"You aren't a collector," I said. "What would you do with them?"

He smiled. "Now, that is an interesting thought: What would I do with them? You've seen them?" I nodded. "Then you can understand their appeal."

"You're a man of business. It's been suggested you want them to give to Hugo Chavez, or that you might keep them to enhance your selling position throughout South America."

"Now, that is a thought, too. Hugo is a very sick man, as everyone knows. He hasn't long to live. I can't see my giving them to him, can you?"

"The legend says in part that they might cure him."

"Perhaps access to them then, if he wants—if it can be arranged."

"But you see these idols on a prominent place on your shelf?"

"I must admit that I do."

"They aren't yours to keep."

"Why not? They certainly don't belong to the Inca, as they no longer exist as a society. The Spanish have no claim to them. From what Kira tells me, they were made in what is now Peru, then discovered almost precisely on the border line between Chile and Argentina. Those two countries are verging on war. Imagine what would happen if their existence became known. How many more would die to possess them? No, like so many things in life, the idols belong to those who have them."

"You won't be allowed to keep them."

"Why not? I'll deny having them. You can say I do, others can say I do, but I'll just deny it. Who's to know? It wouldn't be the first time. But…"

"Yes?"

"I've not made up my mind. There is a downside to my having them, I must admit. And what you said yesterday about friends in Washington struck a chord. If it's believed I have these idols, I lose any chance of mending some fences, and I don't want to jeopardize my access to some of the toys that make this expedition possible.

I was only just able to get them this time; I'd like unfettered access to them hereafter. In many ways, they are the future."

"You want me to pass that along?"

"Why, no, not at all. I haven't yet made up my mind, and the weather waits for no man. While your proposition is intriguing I need time and I must leave here shortly. Kira and Carlos will be joining me while I consider just what it is I intend to do."

"Anyone else?"

"Stern may come."

"Why is that?"

"I could use some good press—at least it better be good." He glanced at his watch. "Consider this: since Kira is coming, so are the idols. You'll know where they are. I've given you all the time I can. I'd really like you to come along. This will be a feather in your cap, so to speak, a winter climb of Vinson Massif. It will be a first, and you'll knock off another of the Seven Summits you pursue. You may never get this chance again. I'll leave it to Bryan. I hope to see you when we set out." He paused, then added, "If you want these idols, or if you want to keep them out of certain hands, then you really have no choice. And I will tell you what I've told everyone: hands off these idols until I've made up my mind—and that will be *after* I've summited."

With that, the meeting was over. Bryan stayed with me as I made my way back to where my gear was kept. Once inside, he asked what I'd decided.

"I guess I'm going. Any chance of getting a message out first?"

He shook his head lightly "I doubt it. I can check for you, but he's got a solid grip on communication. Let me help you with your things. We'll go to the shelter with the vehicles and pick one out for you. Let me say, Scott, that I'm personally glad you're coming."

"Why's that?"

"I've got a bad feeling about the mix of characters on this little party. Come on. I think you'll like what you see."

Six

Outside, the Ilyushin IL-76 was taxiing to the runway. The jet engines whined at near full pitch just as we reached an oversized shelter. We paused at the entrance to watch the plane race down the runway then lift sharply into the ebony sky, four yellow streams blazing from the engines, navigation lights blinking. I felt an unexpected stab of isolation unlike any I'd ever experienced before.

I considered it as we went through the double doors…then put my finger on it. I'd never before been so utterly at the mercy of one man's whim. Ainsworth was an arms dealer, and though Bryan said these men were military or ex-military, they were—by another definition—mercenaries. We were as isolated here as if we were on Mars. And though the technology promised to make this expedition possible, the elements were unforgiving in the extreme, beyond the innovation of man. Any mistake, a single misjudgment, or an abrupt change in weather and we'd all perish, frozen in place like the doomed Robert Scott expedition. It was found and buried where they died in 1912. It was a frightening thought.

The shelter, I saw, was perhaps half again the size of the ones in which I slept and dined. Lined up precisely down the middle was the most exotic machinery I'd ever seen. Picture something very sleek and space-age—like from a science fiction magazine—and you'll have an idea what I was looking at.

They were gray and black, perhaps twelve feet in length, five across. The forward portion was dominated by a clear bubble where the driver sat. Behind him, like the body of a snail, lay the smooth sides and flat top of the vehicle that enclosed the engine and fuel. Each vehicle was propelled by six oversized tires, resembling inner tubes, three on each side.

"What are they?" I asked, a bit in rapture at what I was seeing.

"ETVs. The Army designates them Extreme Temperature Vehicles—Experimental. Each wheel is independently supported and powered. It's all connected to a very sophisticated computer system that assures traction in most any condition. We've got an even dozen of this single-seat number in this shelter. There are eight double-man units in the adjoining shelters. They're five feet longer. The passengers sit in tandem, a bit like in a jet fighter. Two other shelters house the sleds that these vehicles will pull in a train, carrying all the gear and fuel we'll need. There's also a squad version that houses four men up front with six above in the rear but we have none of those."

"I take it that they're snowmobiles of some sort?"

"Only superficially. They are an original design from the snow up, constructed of polymers, titanium, and special alloys. They're designed to operate at more than 100 degrees below zero. Keep in mind that the coldest temperature ever recorded on earth is minus 128 degrees Fahrenheit"

"What's the fuel?"

"Believe it or not, ordinary gasoline. Well, not so ordinary. Some agents have been added to make it more hospitable at extreme low temperatures, but even absent that, gasoline is the fuel of choice in these conditions. For all practical purposes it doesn't freeze, at least not on earth. In this case, they drive rotary engines that give a much higher power ratio than does a reciprocating engine, and their design makes them far less prone to freeze up. There's also virtually no vibration, which makes riding in these things almost a pleasure."

"Range?"

"Three hundred miles, plus. If you add a fuel sled to the train, you can extend that two, three even four times. And quiet. The military required they be virtually silent, since sound carries so well across snow." He moved to the first one and tilted the bubble forward to give me a view inside. There was a single, comfortable looking seat with a standard brake and accelerator pedal on the floor. The steering device was a wheel. "You don't straddle the engine but sit comfortably here. The interior's heated, obviously. In fact, you can make it dangerously hot."

"How's that?"

"You could go out there in your skivvies if you wanted to be in complete comfort; that's how much heat the operator compartment can be made to generate. But if you broke down and the engine stopped, you'd be dead within minutes. So we'll travel in proper gear and keep the temperature within the bubble at just above freezing."

"How fast is it?"

He smiled. "At 250 horsepower, fast enough to get you in trouble. We'll be practically running at idle, going at a steady 10 to 30 miles an hour, depending on conditions and how far we have to go. Given the climb in elevation, we don't want to push it for everyone. People need to adjust."

"Why so much horsepower?"

"The military product will be armored, of course, and though the new stuff is relatively light weight, armor will add weight to the basic machine. They're also meant to trail a long train of supplies and equipment. There are, as well, sealed sleds for soldiers. And though I've not been told, my guess is you can mount weaponry directly on these things, specially designed or modified for extreme cold weather use. The back, you'll notice, is designed like a platform. You can picture for yourself what could go there."

I could. There was room for a heavy gun and at least two men on top.

I walked around the closest one, running my fingers across the very slick surface. The skin was unlike any material I'd ever touched before, almost oily in texture. "So I'll be driving one of these?"

"Right. They're simple to operate, but I'll give you a briefing before we set out." Men were filing in behind us. "Time to go. They're going to move these out and hook up the train. They're already loaded up. We should go the dining room for the briefing."

～～～

Esmeralda and Ignacio had set up the tables for a presentation. Seated facing them were Kira and Carlos. Zapata was in the middle, with Stern at the other end. I sat between them.

If Esmeralda was unhappy with the sudden change she didn't show it. "Welcome to the expedition. We will be setting out for Vinson Massif in about two hours. I want to give you an overview, since you did not receive the original material. In a summer climb we would normally fly from here to Camp One in a Twin engine Otter. But that isn't possible, given the special vehicles we need for the winter assault of Vinson Massif. We're covering a short distance this first day to let everyone adjust and learn how to operate the ETVs and for Bryan's men to confirm that the ETVs are functioning properly. We'll rise just 800 feet in elevation, and the route is almost entirely flat. It should be easy and will give you plenty of time to adapt to your own ETV. Be cautious with them. They are capable of far more than we'll be using them for, and you could get yourself in trouble by being reckless."

"Just why are there enough for so many of us?" Stern asked suspiciously. "That doesn't make sense."

"The ETVs are not in production as yet. They brought an excess along because they've never been used in these conditions previously. They've been tested, but that's not the same thing. And we have no idea how extreme the weather will be. We'd only planned to take one of the tandem ETVs, for example, just to give it a trial in actual conditions. Bryan is bringing seven of his crew, so with the addition of so many, there'll be two of his people to a double ETV, as those are a bit more demanding to operate. My brother and I will be in the one we were planning to use all along. In all, there will be 12 ETVs—seven singles, five doubles. All the gear we need will be pulled in sleds by the doubles, which have more power.

"Camp One is at 7,000 feet. We'll spend tonight there, then leave tomorrow for Camp Two, which is at 12,800 feet. This is usually designated as Camp Three, but we'll go straight there tomorrow, bypassing the usual second camp. The following two days are for acclimatization to the new altitude. We don't want any trouble with high altitude sickness or related problems. Those of you just down from Aconcagua won't need it, but the rest of us do. The next day, weather permitting, is summit day. Vinson Massif is 16,050 feet. We will take the single-rider sleds plus the tandem Ignacio and I will be in. We estimate we can get within 300 meters of the summit using them, as it is along a steadily rising and smooth incline, but that will depend on the local snowfall conditions. We may not get that close, but I don't expect to be that far off. We'll park the ETVs and climb to the summit from there, then back to the vehicles for the return to Camp Two for celebration."

"How long will we be out of the snowmobiles?" Kira asked.

"These vehicles are scarcely snowmobiles. Roundtrip on foot could be as little as two hours."

"What will we wear?" Zapata asked.

"Suits as specialized as the ETVs. You will find them equally exotic." She went on to explain shelter assignments and how our bathroom needs would be seen to. This was always an issue on climbs, but the extreme temperatures this time made that doubly so.

"How many days, round-trip, are planned?" Zapata asked.

"If these conditions hold, we should be back here in six days," Ignacio said, standing up. "But I wouldn't count on it. Weather here is never stable for long, and this region is well known for its windy conditions. That's why we're planning on ten days."

"But we can do it in six?" Carlos asked.

"That's our intention. Perhaps, for once, it will actually go that way." He paused. "There is something else. Beginning today, each of you will take one azithromycin pill every day." That was the generic name for Zithromax, a very powerful antibiotic. "This is in addition to the supplement you've all been given to offset the effects from lack of sunlight."

"Why?" Carlos demanded. "Is this about that dead scientist?"

"He died?" Stern asked, looking shocked. Carlos nodded.

"That's absurd," Ignacio answered. "He was very sick, that is true, but I was assured that he was quite alive when they put him on the plane earlier. The pill is just a precaution, since we don't know what he had or whether it was communicable."

"If it was a virus, an antibiotic is a waste of time," Kira said.

"We do what we can with what we have." He looked us all over. "Perhaps this is a good time to ask if are you all certain you want to do this? Esmeralda and I have worked to make it possible to add so many at the last minute, but only Señor Devlon is an experienced climber. The rest of you have no significant history at this. And while it is our hope that all will go well, we will encounter very difficult conditions."

Kira laughed in an especially nasty way. "We're going because Mr. Ainsworth insists. It's not like any of us has a choice."

"And how hard can it be?" Stern said. "We're driving sealed snowmobiles almost to the top. I think it'll be fun."

"Let us hope so. All right," Esmeralda answered, "you all need to suit up. Follow us."

Bryan was waiting for us inside still another shelter. He came over to me while two of his men, plus Esmeralda and Ignacio, helped the others.

The suits were on racks, which gave them the appearance of space age scarecrows. The outer layer was white, and for this expedition bordered with strips of shiny silver, a bit bulky in appearance, topped with a round helmet. They reminded me very much of the Apollo astronaut space suits I'd seen pictures off. Across them, front and back, was a pattern of faded, though reflective, colors to give each a distinct appearance.

"Are you familiar with the Extended Cold Weather Clothing System the Army's come up with?" he asked.

I shook my head. "Before my time. I just wore a parka and an extra pair of socks."

"The WCS, as it's known, is designed to allow soldiers to fight at 60 degrees below zero. It's multilayered. I won't go into the details, but it's got, like, two dozen pieces of clothing, every set made of different material. The concept is that you mix and match as necessary."

"Like in climbing."

"Right. This is another generation altogether." He took a box from a stack, removed the top, and lifted out what looked like my grandfather's long johns. "Leave your underwear on—but nothing else. Put this against your skin. It will cover you entirely, except for your face and hands. Your face will be protected by the helmet. You'll put on a pair of special reheating gloves, then you'll wear an ETES, Extreme Temperature Excursion Suit, which you see here. It's got boots and gloves, as well. The whole arrangement is a bit bulky but surprisingly comfortable."

"How does it keep me warm?"

"Don't ask me to explain it in detail, but in theory it couldn't be simpler. First, there's this outer, protective layer." He fingered it. "Within it is insulation—not enough on its own, you understand—but it protects you a bit when you go from heat to cold. To keep you alive, the suit regulates itself to a proper temperature. There is no outside or artificial source of heat. It relies entirely on your body for that. The trick, I was told, is that this stuff," he laid back the outer layer of the spacesuit to expose an inner lining. "It simply won't let your body heat escape unless you want it to. See these controls on your left sleeve forearm?" He lifted the suit's arm. "You use them to adjust to comfort. It works by releasing heat. I'm told that in tests these things have gone to minus 130 degrees, a temperature colder than any found on earth, and the test subjects were able to adjust them to the point where they were hot inside. The material is originally a NASA development. I can tell you that the first time I used one I was pretty toasty. The control actually self-regulates to adjust to our metabolism, but you can override as you want. It's really simple."

"I can't imagine how much all this costs. Ainsworth's certainly no penny pincher."

"Not when he wants something. He's all in with this expedition. Let's get you dressed."

I stripped down to my skivvies, then climbed into the long johns. Bryan put my gear into a duffle bag with my name on it. He pulled the hood up over my neck and head, then adjusted it around my cheeks, chin and forehead. He handed me a pair of gloves, which I immediately slipped on. "Boot size?" he asked. I told him, and he pulled a pair out of a box and set them aside.

The suit divided around the middle. First I climbed into the bottom half, then sat on a chair while I slipped on the boots, which he then sealed to the suit's legs. "Once you're all set, do a bit of walking. Make sure the boot size is right, but they're well padded. You only have to be close for them to give a good fit. The bottom is specially designed to grip ice at extreme temperatures and, of course, if needed, you'll use crampons."

Next he slipped the top half over my head, waiting for me to wiggle myself into a comfortable fit, then sealed the suit together around my waist. I estimated that the ETES skin was no more than a half inch in thickness in most places, a bit more in others. There was some padding at the knees, elbows and posterior to protect from wear. I envisioned Kevlar inserts eventually included in key position for military use, but there was none of that now.

He handed me the outer gloves. "Put these on when you get ready to go outside. The same with the helmet. I'll help if you need it, but all you do is pull it on, face open, then snap it to the collar. Like this. You'll know when you've got it right. To remove it, place both hands, one on each side, and press inward. You'll feel the contact release. Then just lift it off. The controls for the face cover are on both sides. The glass or plastic—or whatever the clear cover is made of—will not fog up. Your tax dollars at work. It's got a built-in light over your forehead that comes on automatically in the dark. Here's the override—in case you want it off for some reason. Look to your left inside the helmet and you'll see a read-out of the exterior temperature, as well as your interior temp and humidity. We'll step outside in a bit and let you get a feel for it."

"What about the air supply?"

"It pulls it from outside, heating it before it reaches the helmet."

"Hearing?"

Bryan grinned. "Now that's *really* clever. The helmet has a sensor that picks up sound and amplifies it to your ears so that the volume and range your ears are accustomed to is reproduced. Pretty nifty."

"How do I handle a private conversation?"

"Here. Turn the hearing device off, then touch your helmet to the helmet of the person you want to talk to. Very private."

"What about power?"

"It doesn't need much, as I understand it, and the power supply has an extended life. It functions primarily off your body heat and movement like a motion watch. But when you're in the ETV there's a plug to your left. Insert it here," he pointed to a spot on the left side of the helmet, "and it will keep the charge up. Let me go check on the others."

I went ahead on my own and put on the helmet, which proved as easy as promised. Carlos was dressed already, as was Zapata. They walked easily to the exit, so I decided it was time to go outside, as well. I slipped on the gloves and walked out behind them.

The suit was surprisingly simple to move in. In fact, it was much less restrictive than the clothing I'd typically wear on a summit day. It was light and comfortable. I felt almost naked, as there was so little between me and the elements. I moved through the double door exit, and as I stepped outside I reached to the side of my helmet and lowered my face cover.

At once I could see that the helmet was limiting. While I could see directly in front of me, my peripheral vision was reduced, and it was necessary to move my body side to side to see properly. My vision upwards was also limited, which meant that on the mountain I'd have to lean slightly backward to see the way ahead and above me, something the military would have to take a look at.

The remarkable aspect of the suit was that I never experienced any significant cold as I stepped into the 40-below-zero night. There was the sensation of coolness across my body, but that soon passed, and I found myself as comfortable as I'd been in the shelter.

The camp, I saw, was buzzing with activity. Lights had been set up outside, grouped in bright clusters that pierced the darkness. The ETVs were now out, arranged in two lines. A mist rose from the rear of each, so I knew they were running—but I couldn't hear a sound from any of them. Bryan's men were connecting sleds to them and turning on running lights as they did.

Other spacemen were walking about as I was joined by the rest of those who'd dressed in this shelter. Ignacio spoke. "Everyone hear me? Good. Just walk about a bit. In a few minutes we'll go to an ETV. I'll show you the ropes, then you can take it for a quick spin. We may look ready to set out, but we've got a good hour to go yet."

In the darkness, I realized that the suits were not entirely white, as they had first appeared. In the darker conditions outside, the patterns I'd also observed that within the shelter they were more distinct, the unique color patterns of each more alive. It made it easier to see us, and the color and design differences made it possible to know one of us from the other.

In the distance, I heard shouting. I turned and saw several men running a bit awkwardly, out of the light into the dark beyond the shelters.

"What's going on?" Stern asked, his voice sounding as natural as if we were in a room together.

Before anyone could answer, a man shouted in the distance. "She's dead."

I broke into a run toward the far end of the camp, where I joined perhaps eight men who were standing in a rough circle. On the snow, lit by several helmet lights, lay the pale white, utterly beautiful and very frozen nude body of Rhea Harsten.

Seven

Esmeralda called the meeting to take place in the dining shelter. Everyone was gathered, looking solemn. No one spoke. Instead, they cast furtive looks about the room as we waited. Ainsworth and Pagan were the last to arrive. Ainsworth removed his mauve parka, then came to the head of the tables, while Pagan assumed his position in a corner.

"As you all know my lovely…Rhea's body was found just a bit ago." Ainsworth's voice was subdued but oddly flat, as if he were discussing an unexpected technical glitch. "We've taken it inside and seen that it is treated properly. Needless to say, I'm stunned by this development. I have no idea what took place. Does anyone have any information about how this could have happened?"

No one was saying if they did. After a long moment, Stern spoke. "When did you see her last?"

Ainsworth considered the question before speaking. "When we went to bed last night. I couldn't sleep—I'm sure you all understand—and went into the common area in my shelter to do some work. Afterwards, I fell asleep on the couch. I've been busy all morning with preparations, as you can imagine, and I never realized she wasn't in our sleeping quarters until her body was found. As you know, she was to remain here for the duration of the expedition. Her sleeping habits have been irregular since we arrived, what with the constant darkness. Not seeing her aroused no concern. Did anyone see her this morning?"

Again, no one answered.

"This is some kind of terrible accident," Ainsworth concluded. "I can only imagine that Rhea took a sleeping pill and wandered outside in a confused state. In these conditions, absent any clothing, death would have been all but instantaneous."

"Are there any signs of foul play?" Stern asked.

Ainsworth gave him a hard look. "None. And this is hardly the time or place for such questions. This is simply a terrible accident."

"What I mean is, is there any bruising? Or signs of rape?"

You have to love Stern; always going for the jugular.

"Don't be absurd," Ainsworth snapped.

"How about needle marks?" Stern persisted.

"Of course not. That's enough of that."

"What plans do you have for her body?" Bryan asked respectfully.

"That's a good question. As I said, she's been tended to. I've had her moved into the cold until we return, then I'll take her back with me after the climb. There is no plane before then. She's from Iowa originally. I'm sure her parents will want to see her buried there."

"Have you notified them?" Bryan asked, but Ainsworth didn't reply.

"Is the expedition still on?" Kira wanted to know, sounding hopeful that it was not.

Ainsworth looked startled at the question. "Why, of course. Rhea understood my dream. She'd want it that way." He glanced at his watch. "We'll set out in one hour."

"It's started already," Stern said the moment we were alone, "and we haven't even left on the climb."

"What's started?"

"The deaths. Betcha this turns out to be a murder. What do you think?"

"Why do you say that?"

"Naked, in the snow? Come on. No one goes out naked in these temperatures unless they are carried out or are running for their life."

"Maybe she was disoriented."

Stern lowered his voice. "She's got a history. She was with him to get clean, from what I hear. She had no access to drugs of any kind here. Ainsworth saw to that. If she took a pill, he gave it to her." He looked around, then said, "They had a volatile relationship. Lots of fights. I'm not the only one who's thinking something funny has happened."

"I don't think your questions endeared you to him."

Stern shrugged. "What do I care? His dodging them was as good as a direct answer."

"I don't recall him dodging all of them. Your timing did seem out of place."

"What? You're on his side now?" Stern looked indignant.

"I'm on no side. I'm just saying you didn't show much tact, did you? And it doesn't really matter, does it?"

"What do you mean?"

"She's dead, and you'll write it up to read just the way you want—regardless of what Ainsworth says."

"Hey!"

"Are you still going on this climb?"

Stern grinned. "I wouldn't miss it for the world. This has got the smell of best-seller written all over it."

⌐⌐⌐

Ainsworth was wrong. It was two hours before we set out, mid-afternoon by my watch. This was turning into a long day. Two of Bryan's men were left in the camp to maintain it until we returned. So there were 17 of us leaving on this stage of the expedition, counting support staff.

Seated in my ETV, I checked the gauges to familiarize myself with them. One, I noted, was a GPS locator. As instructed, I plugged myself into the power source. There wasn't much to do after that until the first ETV finally set out. Esmeralda came on the radio to inform us we were leaving and to watch our distance one from another.

Esmeralda and her brother in a tandem led the way, followed by Ainsworth. After him were Kira, Carlos, Stern, Zapata, Pagan and myself. We were trailed by the remainder of the tandem ETVs with the support staff, each pulling a long train of supplies. Bryan brought up the rear. Our headlights stretched out in a steady stream forward, causing the darkness beyond to be even more pervasive than usual. It was as though we were on another planet, moving slowly through a frozen, alien landscape. Inside, I was in comfort; out there, without the protection of technology, was a frozen death.

The machine, I found, was a joy to operate and ride in. The clear bubble canopy offered an outstanding view in front and to both sides. The giving, oversized tires cushioned what irregularities the vehicle encountered and provided excellent traction at this point. The ETV was remarkably stable and smooth in operation, and very quiet. The interior temperature had been set for 36 degrees. I kept my visor open but was still completely comfortable. The self-adjusting suit maintained my body at an optimal temperature.

I held the recommended ten-foot distance from Zapata. Esmeralda, or Ignacio, whichever one was driving their tandem ETV, and we began with a steady pace of just five miles per hour. At about the half-hour mark we gradually sped up until we were moving at ten miles per hour. I judged that the pace was a reflection of the newness of the machinery and a consideration for the tandem ETVs that were pulling sleds. Because the snow pack was solid and even, it was initially like motoring across a vast white blanket spread over a parking lot.

Not everyone found the vehicle as easy to operate as I did. Kira, I noticed, had difficulty maintaining her distance. She'd tailgate, then drop back too far, then race up to tailgate again. I assumed this was her usual driving technique on paved roads. She also had some trouble steering a straight course, tending to swing more left and right than anyone else.

Though I understood that we could, in theory, communicate with one another, Esmeralda limited contact from her to us individually, and from us to her alone. I couldn't hear what anyone else had to say. We'd been warned that we'd not stop unless it was necessary, and the first time we did was nearly a disaster.

We halted to consider the way ahead around an expanse of rugged ice. Kira didn't realize that Esmeralda had stopped, so she plowed into the rear of Ainsworth's ETV. I couldn't hear the exchange because of the radio situation, but I saw him climb out of his vehicle and inspect it for damage. Kira popped open her bubble and the two spoke for a long heated minute before he went back into his ETV and she buttoned up. A moment later, we set out on the detour.

I found my situation to be very strange. I was setting out on a climb I really didn't want to make and had no intention of doing if I could avoid it. I hoped that I'd have a shot at Ainsworth in camp that night. The sooner I neutralized the idols, the happier I'd be. I'd given up any practical thought of taking them myself. In this remote region, without allies, that would be impossible. As for climbing Vinson Massif, Ainsworth had assumed that to do so was my personal quest and for that reason I'd want to go with him. It wasn't, but if I ever did plan it, I'd climb in the summer the standard way, not like this. For any real mountaineer, this expedition was surreal.

While I enjoyed the ultra-sleek science fiction-ish vehicle I was driving, I had no stomach for this expedition. It was unnatural, though technology in climbing was unavoidable—and much of it had become indispensable. On nearly all peaks there was ready communication. Even if there were no cell towers for cell phones— and there sometimes were—two-way radios were generally effective. But even in the most remote regions satellite telephones allowed communication, either with separate parts of an expedition or with the outside world.

When I'd first begun climbing, one of the realities—and one of the appeals—had been the isolation that came with mountaineering. That was now largely a thing of the past. I'd heard a cell phone ring on Elbrus in Russia and on Mt. McKinley in Alaska. I'd watched climbers texting on Everest. Stern had filed his blog from the mountain.

Here, of course, we were all but completely cut off. I assumed that Esmeralda had a sat phone and was certain Ainsworth did.

Bryan likely had one, as well, and all his team would have a form of communication with him, though I'd not seen any obvious signs of it.

Over the years, there'd been steady improvements in climbing gear and clothing—incremental, for the most part—but some of them had really altered things. Light-weight clothing had been one welcome change, along with tents that could withstand almost any gale. Crampons and expanding pitons had made summiting easier than it had once been.

But most of all there'd been a change in climbing ethics. At one time, only skilled mountaineers attempted the demanding peaks. But all this new technology made it increasingly easy for most fit athletes with a bit of time on their hands and too much money to climb any mountain. Where once *how* you summited was at least as important as the fact that you had, now it didn't seem to matter. On Everest, some climbers flew to Base Camp by helicopter, though only those with deep pockets eliminating the long approach march that was so demanding. Drugs were used to increase blood count. And in some cases, Sherpa were short-roped to a climber, in effect pulling the climber to the summit.

The desire to climb Everest and an obsession by some to climb each of the Seven Summits had altered mountaineering I'd learned to love all those years ago with my grandfather. Adventurer Dick Bass had created the Seven Summit challenge and was the first to accomplish it. The publicity surrounding his achievement had propelled people from all walks of life to seek the challenge.

Mockery was the word for what Ainsworth was doing here. This was a stunt. There was no valid reason for climbing Vinson Massif in the dead of winter. I'd just climbed Aconcagua in winter, though not by choice. As a climber I considered it to be showing off, creating an artificial challenge for bragging rights. I'd done it only because I'd been on a mission just peripherally connected with the climb itself, and I was only here to complete that mission.

Climbing Vinson Massif in these conditions was simply impossible by ordinary standards. Almost everything used in the summer climb here wouldn't function or perform satisfactorily this time of year. Special equipment was mandated at almost every level. And not just any special equipment, but state of the art, space-age curiosities developed for NASA or the military. Most of all, it required money in quantities I could scarcely imagine.

Then there was this: Ainsworth had gone out of his way to pressure a large number of us who had no desire to climb this mountain to come along. I had seen hints of why this was so and didn't like it a bit. He was clearly enjoying the power he wielded over us. As he was the key decision maker in the equation, he would be the focus of our attention.

But there was no need for us to be in such a remote region to conduct business. He could have made his decision about the idols in Punta Arenas, certainly at Patriot Hills. I could think of no reason for him to drag us all off into the most distant part of the earth like this.

No good reason, that is.

⌖⌖⌖

The wind kicked up after the first two hours, and the terrain became more demanding. I glanced at the outside temperature. It registered minus 60 degrees Fahrenheit. I didn't want to think what it was like with the wind chill. Inside the ETV I remained comfortable, but the vehicle was buffeted on occasion, enough to remind me how nasty it was outside. The wind also kicked up snow, obscuring visibility.

Now the going was more difficult and we stopped several times. Twice I spotted Esmeralda and Ignacio exit their ETV and walk ahead. After a delay of some duration they'd return and Esmeralda would announce a course correction. We bypassed what was described as a crevice, though in these conditions I could not see it. Three other times we took detours around rough terrain that would have proven difficult for the ETVs with sleds. All this served to reduce our pace.

The wind eased and there was no more blowing snow. It was seven o'clock when we came to a stop just below the Branscombe Glacier, the traditional location of Camp One—or Low Camp, as it was sometimes known. I pulled my ETV to the right of the

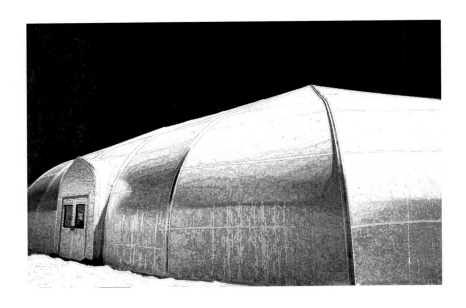

line to park it, as instructed, and remained inside with the engine running while I watched the tandem ETVs with their supply trains pull ahead and into position.

I was stiff and grateful to be able to move about and stretch, even though I was still inside the ETV. Using the light from our vehicles, as well as from theirs, Bryan's men climbed out in their space suits and set up a ring of bright lights. Then they set about erecting camp. It was a miracle of precision.

First to go up were two extended, barrel-shaped shelters very much like those we'd used at Base Camp, though they possessed a certain luminescent quality the others lacked. They were in place in less than half an hour. One would house the ETVs, the other the sleds and whatever supplies weren't used elsewhere.

Those where we'd eat and sleep went up next, and these were very different. I'd once attended a hot-air balloon festival and had arrived before sunrise. I'd watched the teams spread out the balloons, then use jetting flames to fill them with heated air. The transition from an expanse of material lying on the grass to floating object was very rapid. The moment enough hot air was inside, they rose quickly in the darkness, then stood towering over us, glowing in gaudy colored patterns.

This was very much like that. These shelters were unlike those at Patriot Hills and were named Mars Atmosphere Habitats, MAH, or to us simply "habitats." They were, as I understood it, based on the projected design for such structures to be used on Mars. They were constructed of a much thinner material than the shelters at Patriot Hills, which resulted in their glowing with a gossamer effect when they were inflated.

They were stretched out cross the snow, then filled with what I assumed was heated air because, like the balloons, they suddenly rose and hung there, glowing. Each was a different shade of pastel: coral, cerulescent, mauve, veriscent, and so on. They were also shaped a bit like hot air balloons, though not in the extreme. They were nearly round, with a flattened, though slightly curved, top. The portion touching the snow was slightly narrower than the body of the shelter. They were the oddest structures for habitation I'd ever seen.

Amazingly, it took less than an hour to get them up and for our supplies to be carried in. Esmeralda gave us our habitat assignments by color, then told us to go inside. I left the ETV running, as instructed. They were never to be turned off when they were anywhere outside of one of the special equipment shelters. I raised the bubble, lowered my visor and stepped out onto the snow, glad finally to be stretching my legs. I was chilled for a minute, then the suit's system rebounded, and once again I found myself in comfort in arctic temperatures.

I was assigned to the green habitat. Behind me, one by one, the ETVs we'd arrived in were driven inside one of the extended shelters by Bryan's men. I understood these were to be maintained at a temperature just above freezing. Before ducking into my habitat I took a last look at our camp.

The glowing, balloon-shaped tinted habitats, the piercing light of the ETV headlamps and lights, the muted sounds, the movement of the climbers and staff in their glistening white space suits—this was one of the most unusual, and beautiful, scenes I've ever witnessed. It was as if taken from a science fiction movie.

I entered through the double door system and was embraced by a rush of warm air.

Eight

I was sharing my habitat with Stern, Bryan, and one of his men, who was still working outside. Bryan was in and out, making certain the camp was secure for our rest period. I couldn't call it night, since we existed in perpetual darkness.

On his last trip in, he brought a hot meal to Stern and me, the food sealed in special containers. As we took them and found our places, I asked how the camp was arranged, as I'd never seen anything like it.

"Simple enough," he said as we began eating, sitting on folding chairs around a specially designed table in the center of the habitat. "Mr. Ainsworth and Angel have their own habitat, the same as this one. Esmeralda and Ignacio have a tent of their own. She's put Kira, Carlos, and two of my men in a third habitat. There's a cooking habitat, where one of my men stays, and the rest of my men are in the equipment habitats as a precaution. Seven habitats and shelters in all."

"How do these things stay warm?" Stern asked. "I don't hear a generator."

"No, eight of the sleds we're pulling are a next-generation fuel cell that's designed to operate at these Mars-like temperatures. One of each is connected to a habitat and provides all the power to heat and inflate them. There's a spare, just in case. The protocol with the ETVs and our supplies is to keep them indoors out of the elements when not operating."

"I take it the semi-balloon shape filled with hot air is what keeps these erect?" I asked.

"That's it. They will only function like this in extremely cold conditions. You can't really tell without taking them apart, but they have a triple wall. The inner layer is almost the same material as the inner lining of our suits."

"What about wind?" I asked.

"I'm told they're good to 80 miles an hour. Even then they are structurally secure, just not stable. They'll lay over or flop around. That's what the manual claims. I don't know that they've ever been in such conditions."

"I seem to recall that winds of 50 miles an hour are common here."

"So I understand." He grinned.

"What if we have higher winds?" Stern asked, clearly concerned.

"In that case, we'll see just how good the design really is. Part of the reason the Army let us have these things is to discover that very thing."

We ate in silence for a time. "This is a very power hungry operation," I suggested.

"You've got that right. Half the sleds are hauling fuel to keep us going. But it's the only way to function in these temperatures. We wouldn't survive without the fuel cells and habitats. We just wouldn't."

"That's reassuring," Stern said. "How's Ainsworth's ETV? It looked like Kira really plowed into him."

"It's all right. I can't imagine how she managed to do that at the low speed we were traveling at."

"I had a rule to never let her get behind the wheel of a car when we were married," Stern remarked. "Why do you think I'm in back of her now? She's the world's worst driver."

"She just nudged him. No harm done."

"Say," Stern said, "what is the real story behind this death?"

For a moment I thought Bryan wasn't going to answer, but then he said, "A tragedy. She was a very special lady."

"Seems a bit raw to keep going, don't you think?" Stern asked.

I cleared my throat, then cautioned, "I should warn you that Stern's interviewing you. He just didn't think to mention it."

"Is that right?" Bryan asked pointedly.

"Hey, I'm just asking…, it's all off the record."

"I doubt it," I said.

Bryan eyed Stern, then said, "To answer your question, on a purely emotional level you could say this was a hard decision, but as Scott here can confirm, you often have to make hard decisions in situations like this. Mr. Ainsworth has spent a considerable fortune to make this climb, and he's only got use of the equipment that makes it possible for a short time. He really has no choice but to go on with it."

"Even though he's heartbroken?" Stern said, a trace of sarcasm in his tone.

"Yes, even then," Bryan said as he finished his plate. He looked at me. "I'm going to do the rounds. Want to join me?"

"Sure."

A few minutes later we suited up and went outside, leaving Stern busy on the table with his notebook. Three of the habitats were dim now, the main lights having been extinguished for sleep. The kitchen habitat was still aglow, as were the habitats for Ainsworth and Esmeralda. Bryan took me to the two of the rectangular shelters that housed the ETVs and sleds. Inside, he briefly spoke to each of his men and seemed satisfied with what he learned.

Back outside, he led me in a perimeter check, unnecessary here but a sign of his military background. I'd often found myself doing the same on climbs late at night. There was a steady breeze blowing, but not enough to kick up any of the snow. He stopped when we were in the darkness, reached up to my helmet and turned off my radio, as he did his. Then he leaned forward and touched his helmet to mine.

"What are you doing here?" I asked him. I'd been wondering when we'd get a chance to talk in genuine privacy. "Why aren't you in Afghanistan?"

"I've already been there, three times."

"This just seems an odd situation for someone like you."

"You can say that again." He paused then added, "You don't know the story?"

"No."

"I thought every Ranger had heard it."

While it was true that Bryan and I had not served in close contact with one another during the campaign, there had been one firefight in particular that had occurred not long after we were air-dropped into Afghanistan. He and I had been cut off from our teams for two hours and fought all but back to back. You might not get to know someone intimately in such a situation, but you learn to trust them with your life. It forms a bond you have to experience to understand. Later, after the fighting was over for us and we were blowing off steam, I'd seen him for a night of drinking in Kabul.

After a bit, he said, "I'd just as soon you keep it to yourself. After my third tour I was assigned to the Army's extreme weather program. They wanted someone who'd actually fought in very cold conditions, as my team had. That's when I met Ainsworth. One of his companies was bidding for participation—not actually manu-facturing any of the gear, you understand, but positioning itself to have an inside track in distribution once the DOD authorized sale beyond our own military needs."

"I guess that's all pretty political."

"You got that right. Rotten through and through, and the men with stars on their shoulders were the most corrupt, all looking for a soft landing after they retired. Anyway, one of them used me to leak some specifications. His name isn't important. He's dead. I was divorced—like most of us—after our second deployment, but I had a really sick son. Anyway, I was told that Ainsworth was going to get the contract regardless, so the data I provided just let him bid a bit cheaper and made it easier for him.

"Well, I should have known better. It all came out. I was allowed to resign in lieu of court martial. I'd seen Ainsworth several times, even spent most of a day with him at one point as I explained the ramifications of some of the designs for the military. He's got a sharp mind, I can tell you. I figured that when I was forced out of the Army and off the project, that would be all she wrote, but I'll give Ainsworth this; he contacted me and paid the medical bills for my son that were part of the original agreement then hired me to put this deal together for him. He's been in the doghouse with DOD ever since the blow up—I guess it was one incident too many—but he's subsidizing this test of the equipment, and he's earning a lot of brownie points for it. That's another reason this expedition is a 'go' no matter what happens."

"I'm sorry to hear all that. I was never involved in procurement, but if your story was commonly known, I think I'd have heard about it."

"That's a plus, then. I've been pretty down ever since separation." Changing the subject, he said, "What do you think of all this?" He used his arm to take in the camp.

"Impressive. This new equipment is revolutionary. Do you think it will hold up?"

"I don't know, to be honest. It's all been tested, but in very controlled conditions, mostly in a laboratory. It'll handle the temperatures, I'm told, but I don't know about the wear and tear." He didn't speak for a bit, then said, "I'm surprised all of you came on board like this at the last second."

"It's not like we had a choice. I'd hoped to see Ainsworth tonight, but that's not going to happen; maybe tomorrow, when we lay over for two days."

"Maybe. He doesn't share his plans with me."

"Have you heard about the Inca idols?"

"A bit here and there. I take it that's what this is all about?"

I explained the significance of the idols, especially in view of Ainsworth's relationship with Hugo Chavez.

"So you're here on behalf of friends." 'Friends' was a euphemism used to mean 'spooks,' as CIA, DIA or other agents were known.

"Why else?" I cautioned him that Zapata was a trained agent and not to be taken lightly. "And Kira's a killer," I added. "Absolutely ruthless, with nothing to lose."

"She's with him right now."

"What?"

"After he ate he sent for her. I think she's spending the night."

"What about Angel?"

"I don't know. Sleeping at the foot of bed? By the door? Maybe it's a threesome."

"I guess he didn't take what I told him about her seriously."

"I guess not."

"And he doesn't seem to be in mourning."

"No, he doesn't, does he?" We stood in silence for a bit then he asked, "How far are you prepared to go with this idol thing?"

"I was willing to start on this so-called climb. I'll talk with him if I ever get the chance and see if I can persuade him to my way of thinking. If getting the contract for all this gear is really important to him I can't see him wanting to make more enemies at DOD. And I'm told these idols are important. If he goes ahead and acquires them and doesn't give them to me, there will be hell to pay. It will be just as bad if he allows Kira and Carlos or Zapata to sell them directly to Chavez or Castro for that matter. But to answer your question, I'm just along to talk to the man. We're cut off out here. I can't see actually trying to take the idols. What would I do then? Are they even here?"

"I'd say so. He saw them at Patriot Hills, and the way Kira keeps one of her bags with her suggests that she holds them close. What do you know about Carlos?" I told him what Esmeralda had said. "I can't say I'm surprised. He's got that look. There's a lot of that going around." I waited for him to explain himself. Instead, he said, "I don't like that he's maneuvered all of you to come onto this climb. It makes no sense. It's true we had the gear for it, but it complicates everything. When I told him that he didn't want to hear it."

"So why *are* we out here, cut off from the world?"

"I'd say your question answers itself. You're here because that's what he wants. You be careful. I've seen him operate before. I've got good men, but I didn't pick all of them. And there's Angel." There was another pause before he continued. "Stern's on to something, Scott. I don't think Rhea's death was an accident."

"What makes you think that?"

"For one thing, I knew her. I've been with Ainsworth over a year a now. When he traveled—which was damn often—he took Angel with him and left me with Rhea. She was a good kid, cursed with great looks. She'd modeled a bit because everyone told her that's what she should do, then she ran into Ainsworth. He swept her off her feet. She was 19 at the time, so how hard could it have been? It's been a rough relationship, I can tell you. He's not violent with her, but he's a control freak, and she didn't take well to it."

"I heard she was a drug user."

"Yeah, until last year she was into prescription pills pretty badly she told me, but then she had a pregnancy scare. She thought the kid would be born with problems. It turned out she wasn't pregnant, but she got off the pills anyway. Don't expect me to understand it, but she loved the guy, wanted to get married, have a family."

"He doesn't look like the settling down type to me."

"No, but he wants a son. I don't even want to think how messed up the kid will be—if he ever gets one. He was thrilled when she told him she was pregnant, and pretty upset, supportive—you know—when it turned out to be a mistake."

"What was she doing here?"

"Two months ago she told me she was pregnant, this time for sure. She was ecstatic."

"Did he know?"

"She told him. He'd cooled on their relationship by then. He was seeing someone else, and there'd been trouble between him and Rhea. In fact, I think she got pregnant because of the other woman. So he wasn't thrilled about it, and when she pressed for him to marry her he kept stalling. It was a busy time, and he was seeing the other woman, an actress, I understand. I told Rhea to be patient, that he wanted a son and he'd come around, but his reaction really hit her hard. They weren't together much, and when they were they fought, so she changed her mind about wanting to marry him. Then he stopped seeing the other woman and said they could set a date. I don't think she believed him. Not long after she lost the baby."

"That was tough."

"Yeah. She got back on the pills, and to answer your question, that's why she was here. He was getting her off the stuff again. That's what he told me anyway."

"This isn't a detox center."

"That thought occurred to me, but he's not a man you contradict."

We stood in silence for a bit. Another habitat turned dim as the occupants went to bed.

"Why do you suspect that something's wrong?" I finally asked.

"She wouldn't go outside naked—just think about it. No, I think he spiked her drink then took her out and dumped her. We'll never know. He'll see to that. You watch, when we get back to Base Camp her body will be gone. They'll say they buried her there or sent her back already. You watch."

"Why would he kill her?"

"She told him they were through last night, that she was sick of his games. She told him that she didn't have a miscarriage; she'd had an abortion. And it had been a son."

Nine

Back in the habitat, I lay in semi-darkness. In the stillness that came with rest, the only sound was the gentle purr of the fuel cell that kept us from freezing to death. Despite what Bryan had told me I slept as soundly as I could ever recall and didn't get up until one of his men brought in our breakfast. I drank coffee, ate heartily, then tended to my needs before suiting up to go outside.

Since it felt like morning and my watch said it was morning, it was disconcerting to step out into night. I'd never been in conditions such as these before and was surprised at how disturbing it all was. We are so accustomed to night and day that continuous night is aberrant. It is no wonder that nuclear submarines cruising underwater maintain a standard day and night schedule. Continuous daytime would have been just as strange. Either was very damaging to your well-being, leading to depression and, in some cases, profound neurological disorders.

I was watching the men bring out the ETVs when Zapata joined me. "Do you know that woman went to him last night?" he said by way of greeting.

"You mean Kira?" I wasn't going to let him know anything I knew.

"Of course. Esmeralda is too much a lady for such things."

"It must be tough to compete with someone who has an edge in inducements."

He snorted. "The whore!" Then he coughed.

One of the ETVs died. There were startled shouts then a white-suited man quickly climbed in and fired it up again, racing the engine, I deduced, since I could see a stiff, heated stream of hot discharge coming from the exhaust even though there was virtually no sound. "Why are you here, Evo?"

"For the same reason you are—the idols. *Presidente* Chavez wants them and is prepared to pay a fair price. I've told Kira and Carlos that. They don't seem interested."

Chavez was working all the angles. "What's Chavez consider a fair price?"

"He's made a generous offer of $1,000,000."

"I think Ainsworth has the edge there."

"He refuses to speak with me. I don't think he fully understands what is at stake here for him."

"And what is that?"

"It should be obvious. Presidente Chavez is a sick man. Everyone knows that he's dying of cancer. He believes the idols will cure him. Such a man is not likely to take no for an answer."

"Your plan is to threaten Ainsworth?"

"Of course not," Zapata said indignantly. "He and *el presidente* are good friends. They have done business in the past and will in the future, God willing. He needs to be reminded of that."

"From what I read, Chavez isn't scheduled to be with us much longer."

Zapata glared at me. "The media exaggerate his condition."

"You know better?"

"I've been assured by *el presidente* himself. Ainsworth needs to seriously consider his position. I understand the woman is demanding he pay her and Carlos $25 million for the idols. The very thought is absurd. If he gets them to me, I will give them to Presidente Chavez. Ainsworth will not be out any money and will win the president's everlasting goodwill. That is worth a very great deal."

"And how, exactly, is he to 'get them' to you?"

"Kira and Carlos are at his mercy," Zapata scoffed. "You can see that. I'm certain that she has them with her. He should just take them."

"I see. You actually believe that those golden statues can cure your man?"

"I do not dispute legends. I have read—and witnessed—too many strange things to question them. But perhaps it is only necessary that *el presidente* believe it. Such belief can be very powerful." He coughed again. "I have a request of you. In the event I fail to see Ainsworth, I want you to repeat what I've told you to him. He must be made to see common sense. This is a dangerous game he is playing."

"Zapata, that's twice you've threatened him. Is that what you want me to tell him?"

"You Americans. Do you think your CIA behaves any differently? Ask your masters there. Just do as I tell you and you will have no need to fear for your life. Do I make myself clear?"

———

Forty-five minutes later the camp was down and the sleds loaded up. It had been an amazingly efficient operation. The weather was holding, just as Ainsworth anticipated, and the breeze from the night before, if anything, was significantly less intense. The camp was ablaze with brilliant light until the sleds were all but ready and hooked to the tandem ETVs. Finally, the lights themselves came down and were put away, the scene remaining lit only by the headlights of the ETVs and the bobbing helmets of the men. Ignacio called out for the rest of us to mount up.

We traveled at a slow speed, and there were no incidents this time. Kira maintained an adequate distance from Ainsworth, though I can't say her control of the ETV was improved. Our route was more rugged and demanding than the day before as we steadily climbed increasing elevation 5,800 feet. Esmeralda led us on several detours from the direct route she had laid out at Patriot Hills.

There were no rest breaks. Survival in these conditions was premised on continuous motion out of our habitats. In that way it what not so different from climbing in the Death Zone of Everest. When we did pause before turning from our route, Esmeralda

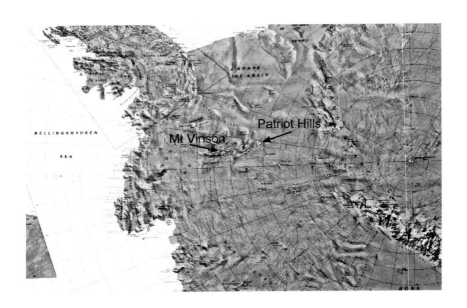

cautioned us all to remain inside. Again, though we could all hear her, we could not hear one another.

I gained an even greater appreciation for the ETV and for my suit. So far, both worked exactly as advertised. I'd never previously had such a comfortable approach trek. In fact, I was sitting so much I feared I'd be a bit out of shape when the actual climbing began. We'd be two days at Camp Two while those who'd not been on Aconcagua acclimatized. The purpose was to avoid edema, blood clots and strokes. I considered asking Esmeralda if she could organize at least one half-day hike just to give our legs a stretch.

But I knew the answer. If she didn't want to risk anyone getting lost during one of these stops, she wasn't going to take a chance on a hike during our acclamation time.

Then I wondered why I'd even considered it. My plan was to talk to Ainsworth and not climb Vinson Massif. In my mind, I wasn't here to climb a mountain—no matter what he thought. But I recalled the vehemence in his eyes when he'd pressed me to come, and I doubted very much that he'd make a deal unless I joined him on the summit assault. In fact, he'd insist on it before giving me an answer. It occurred to me that, depending on the other factors influencing him, electing to go might be my trump card because, all things considered, I just couldn't see him buying these idols. It seemed to me that he had a choice between buttering up Chavez or playing ball with the Department of Defense. I couldn't see how he could do both. Kira wasn't a real contender in my view.

My conversation with Bryan troubled me. One firefight and a drinking bout didn't mean I knew him well, but there was a certain bond between us that I could not lightly dismiss. I'd not heard of his troubles in the Army but could understand them. There were enormous temptations in certain military situations. In my experience, they'd come after combat, when artifacts of antiquity were easily available if you were so inclined. I'd heard rumors of soldiers getting rich from Afghanistan and Iraq loot.

Procurement was another rich source of unethical and illegal money. Every edge a company could get was worth millions. It was a game Ainsworth would be skilled in, and Bryan, being an amateur, had got caught in the middle.

What was I to make of his suspicion that Ainsworth had killed Rhea? He'd been quick to reach that conclusion, and it made as much sense as any other if you believed Ainsworth was that kind of man. Frankly, a drug overdose struck me as the most likely explanation.

It was early afternoon by my watch when Esmeralda informed us that we'd reached Camp Two. At 12,800 feet, it was just 3,250 feet below the summit of Vinson Massif. Again we single ETVs drew up in a ragged line while the tandem versions formed to shine their headlights on the designated site. The exterior lights came out to set the scene fully alight, then, in a very short time, the ETV and equipment shelters were up, as were each of our habitats. Esmeralda told us to go to the one assigned to us and to leave our vehicle running.

Outside, I spotted Ainsworth, standing beside his ETV with Esmeralda and Ignacio. The purple pattern on his suit, I realized, closely resembled a crown. I walked toward him, hoping to arrange a time to meet with him. Instead, I was intercepted by Pagan.

"Mr. Ainsworth is not to be interrupted," he said, very unpleasantly. "If he decides to see you he will let you know." Unlike in the movies, there was no interior light to show me his face. The glare from the brilliant lights reflected off his visor and obscured his features. I supposed it was the same with me.

"I need to talk to Mr. Ainsworth about these stolen idols and the murders on Aconcagua. I'm not certain he understands the severity of the situation or its adverse implications for him if he makes the wrong decision."

"When he decides to see you he will let you know." Pagan stood blocking my way.

"We need to speak." I turned away and walked to my habitat, where I found Stern already in place.

"Those ETVs are something, aren't they?" he said as he stripped off his suit. It was remarkable how quickly the interior of the habitat was warm. The beds, chairs, tables and interior wall I'd noticed before remained quite cold for a time, but they, too, eventually warmed to room temperature. I removed my suit and placed it on its stand.

"I don't want to think about how much they cost."

"You aren't paying for it," he said, "so what do you care?" It was just the two of us for now. "Say, I saw Kira coming out of Ainsworth's hab this morning. She's giving him the full court press. Probably trying to make up for her little incident."

Though his manner was casual, there was the slightest tremor in his voice. "It's to be expected, I suppose," I answered. "There's a great deal at stake for her. The storm on Aconcagua won't last indefinitely. At some point, authorities are going to establish that murders did take place and who committed them. I don't buy Ainsworth's argument that this is going to be hushed up. She needs to get this deal closed."

"What I don't understand is why Carlos is here? It doesn't make any sense that he'd throw away his life at Punta de Inca like that. I...I know what she's got that gets men going, but I can't see that being enough, not for a man like him. She's asking him to abandon his entire life, his business, family, friends. I just don't see it."

I considered it a moment, then decided to tell him what Esmeralda had said, leaving out the personal connection involving her murdered brother.

"So that's it!" Stern said, his eyes lighting up. "I knew there was more to this. Nazis, huh? That's great. Just great. I told you there'd be Nazis! I can feel another best-seller coming on."

～～～

Because we'd be here for two days—and perhaps for a third on return from the summit—Bryan's men set up a dining and meeting habitat, which glowed auburn and was slightly larger than the ones we slept in.

The evening meal was served in two shifts. Bryan and his team ate first, followed by the rest of us, except for Ainsworth. It was awkward, to say the least. Either Carlos or Kira had taken a shot at Zapata, Stern, Fowl and myself just a few days ago. The bullet had struck Lucio, who fell where he stood. We'd been forced to scramble for shelter and been unable to help him as he lay in the line of fire. We'd been forced to watch him slowly bleed to death.

Lucio been Maria Sabato's uncle, and he'd been murdered just a few hours after I'd watched Kira kill his niece. A bit later she had shot at Stern in an offhanded way meant to stop any pursuit but one that could be just as deadly as a carefully aimed round. Finally, Zapata, who'd been part of the team pursuing Kira and Carlos, had turned on us and shot Fowl. As I say, the situation was awkward for everyone, even surreal.

The initial consequences were quiet conversations. Esmeralda made a few polite comments and other attempts at small talk. She had to keep it going on her own, though, as it wasn't catching on.

Zapata coughed several times. Finally I asked how he felt—out of concern for my own health rather than for his.

"Not good," he said. "My throat is killing me, and I'm having some difficulty breathing. Does anyone know the symptoms that scientist had?" Ignacio ran them down for him. "And you say he was dead when they put him on that plane?" He directed that last at Carlos.

"Oh yes, he was very dead. His face was covered. It was like a funeral. You shouldn't be here with us if you are sick."

"I suppose you're right. I'm going back to my habitat and lie down."

"I'll check on you later," Esmeralda said. "We're here for two days. Just rest. It's probably nothing more than the dry air."

As I was working on my final cup of coffee and considering what I'd do with the rest of the evening, two men entered. One was Pagan, the other Ainsworth. Once he had removed his jacket Ainsworth went to the head of the table. Pagan stood off to the side. He was a bullish man, stout, obviously strong, with a large, fleshy face, its features small and clustered towards the middle. His dark eyes took each of us in as if we were slabs of meat.

"This stop is unnecessary for those of you who just climbed Aconcagua," Ainsworth announced, "but for the rest of us it is a safety precaution. The good news is that the weather is holding. I'll limit our stay to one day if I see a change in the pattern, as I'm told these can happen very quickly. I've been taking Diamox to build up my blood count, so this may not even be necessary, but better to be cautious. It's possible we have extra. Check with Esmeralda."

"I'd like to talk to you again," I said.

Ainsworth flashed that disturbing smile. "There will be plenty of time for talk when we return from the summit. That goes for all of you. I understand you each have something you want from me. That is not an unusual position for me to be in. I have important decisions to make, as I do every day, but for now I'm focused on this climb."

"You must know by now that in dealing with Kira you are dealing with a murderer? That Carlos is her accomplice?" I persisted. I didn't care at this point who heard me.

Carlos hissed and turned his face toward me with a look of pure evil.

"The storm over Aconcagua is continuing," Ainsworth said. The nervous tick had returned to his eye. "No one is going into the mountains. The roads are closed. Chile and Argentina are on military alert. The situation there is unchanged and will remain so for some days or weeks. So, in truth, I 'know' nothing."

"Scott is the killer," Carlos said, pointing his finger at me. "We've already told you that. I don't know why he killed those people, but I have my suspicions. We've warned you about him already. He's an assassin with the CIA. He's trying to put the blame on me and Kira; we have done nothing wrong. We have what he wants, and he is just trying to divert attention from himself."

Ainsworth spread his hands before him. "You see? There is more than one version of events, Scott. For now, we'll remain in this camp. Then you are all joining me in the climb." He smiled again. "Enjoy your time here, though there is really nothing to see in this immensity, surrounded by night. Tomorrow I'm planning a little gathering for you all here after dinner. Until then."

With that he donned his gear and, along with Pagan, left us.

After a pause, Stern said, "Esmeralda, do you have any special word on this sickness? Do we need to be concerned? How many of the other scientists are sick?"

Ignacio answered. "To my knowledge, no one else. The scientists thought their colleague had the flu. Nothing more. And I was assured that he was not dead when he boarded that plane."

Carlos scoffed at the comment but said nothing.

"What if it's some exotic bug from the past, frozen in time? Something we modern humans have no immunity to? Has anyone thought about that?" Stern looked around the table for support.

"As usual, Quentin," Kira said, "your imagination is running away with you."

"Those guys are collecting bugs to use in biological warfare, I tell you," he said, raising his voice. "I've read about it! We could already be infected!"

"Don't be absurd," Esmeralda said as she stood. "I want all of you to stay in your habitats. There is nothing to see out there. There are small hills on two sides, which partially shields us from the wind. Bryan's team will be examining and conducting tests on the suits tomorrow. Be certain to tell them of any problems you've had. The next day they'll check all the ETVs."

"When do we leave on the summit attempt?" Carlos asked, sounding genuinely excited at the prospect.

"The day after that, following breakfast."

"How long will the climb take?"

"I'm not certain how far we can ride the ETVs. I believe we can get them to within a few hundred meters of the summit, but it will depend on snowfall. We're not going to take any chances. The best situation would be a day lasting four to five hours. That's if everything goes as planned. But it could take us eight hours if we have to hike an extended distance. In the summer, we summit from this spot in four hours. We then return by foot to a lower camp. The day typically lasts ten hours. This will be much easier because of the technology we have for support. For now, I suggest you all turn in and get some rest."

As I stood up, Kira approached me. "Stay. We need to talk."

Ten

Stern gave us an odd look as he dressed to leave. Everyone filed out while the two cooks cleared the tables then retired to the kitchen area.

"This is nonsense, what you're up to," Kira said, leaning toward me across the table. She was wearing makeup this morning, attempting to look her best, but the strain of these last days showed itself. During that time she had descended from Aconcagua in a rush and become a murderess. "I've got the idols and I'm selling them to Robert. There's nothing you can do to stop it."

I couldn't help but notice the use of the phrase 'I've got' instead of 'We've got' and wondered how Carlos felt about that. "Then why are you worried?" I said.

She made a face. "I'm *not* worried. I just don't want to see you waste your time, is all."

"It's mine to waste."

"Look," she said in a lower voice and leaning forward, "you don't know Robert, but *I* do. I've gotten to know him very well. There's a reason he wants to get Quentin alone up there. You understand? And if you insist on coming, you could get the same medicine. Do you know what I'm saying?"

"You're saying he plans to kill Stern?"

"Not Robert personally. He wouldn't get his hands dirty. But Quentin wrote some very nasty things about him, and now he's got

a chance to settle the score in a place where it can't come back on him. He's in a very tough business, so I doubt this is a new situation for him. That's why Angel is here, you understand?"

"That's some friend you've got. You don't really think you're going to get away with this, do you?"

She straightened. "I'm not getting away with anything. I've got a product and he wants it. It's a straight business deal."

"Has it occurred to you that he can just take the idols? Who's to stop him? His thug's got more than one use."

"He wouldn't do that."

"And why not?"

She paused before speaking. "This needs to be a clean sale for him. He's got trouble enough buying them without rumors going around that he stole them."

I laughed. "You don't honestly believe that, do you? You really think this guy's worried about a few rumors? If that's what you're hanging your future on you need to rethink everything." She eyed me steadily. "If I were you," I continued, "I'd be wondering if he wasn't giving you the same treatment as your ex-husband. You may have slept with him, but that doesn't make you important. Look what happened to Rhea."

"What about Rhea? You're saying he killed her?"

"Why not? She crossed him, and I can accept murder before I can the idea that she ran outside naked in these temperatures." Kira licked her lips nervously. "And what about your Bavarian Nazi buddy? How loyal do you think he's going to be once you've got your hands on the cash? My guess is, he's keeping a close eye on those idols. He doesn't need you, not now, but he sure as hell needs them."

"Nazi? What are you talking about?"

"You need to do your homework before you go to bed with someone. This isn't college. Talk to Ignacio or Esmeralda about it, if you don't believe me. That man has a history you need to know about."

She shook her head, as if to shake off the suggestion. "Just listen to me, Scott. I'm selling those idols, then I'm out of here. Nothing and no one is going to stop me. Surely you understand that. You should return to Base Camp and wait for the next plane. Stay out of this, or you're liable to end up like Quentin."

"Are you planning to warn him?"

She sniffed. "Oh, you'll tell him, though I'd rather you didn't. It will solve some problems for me, you know?"

"It gets easier, doesn't it?"

"What?"

"Killing people, or standing aside and letting them get killed. Why'd you shoot Maria? What possible threat was she to you?"

Kira stood up. "She got in my way, just like you."

<center>~~~~</center>

Back in my habitat, I lay restlessly in bed. I'd warned Stern, telling him about my conversation with Kira, but he'd shrugged it off. "Ainsworth needs me," he said. "He'd like some good PR from this. He doesn't want a bunch of dead people. That's ridiculous. It's the worst possible outcome for him."

"That's pretty tenuous logic to hang your life on. We've got one body already and under suspicious circumstances," I reminded him.

"All the more reason not to have another," he answered flippantly. "Look, Scott, he's trying to get back in good with the DOD. He doesn't want trouble here. Trust me in this. I understand the guy. You know what I think? I think Kira's projecting. She wants me dead, so she thinks he does."

"Maybe she can persuade him to her way of thinking, assuming the man isn't there already."

Stern gave me that cockeyed grin of his. "She's good, but she's not *that* good in the sack."

After that I nodded off intermittently but never fell into a deep sleep. I don't know if it was the way things were shaping up or my body's reaction to interminable darkness. My inability to sleep didn't matter, it turned out, because shortly after midnight Bryan entered the habitat, cold air rushing in with him. He touched my shoulder. He was still wearing his suit and helmet. "You'll want to see this, Scott."

"What's that?"

"Ignacio's dead."

Most of the military types were gathered about a figure lying just beyond the perimeter of the camp. It was lit with the lights from their helmets, casting the scene in stark white and black. I didn't see Ainsworth this time, or Pagan.

"What happened?" I asked as we reached them.

"It looks like his suit was sliced open," Bryan said. "From the condition of the snow, I'd say there was a struggle. Maybe that's when it happened."

"Or maybe it was sliced first and he was held here to freeze to death."

"That, too."

I moved closer. Ignacio's frozen face was fixed in a mask of exertion and pain, so he'd been struggling to the very end. Death by freezing is reported to be easy, almost peaceful after a certain point, as the victim slowly descends into oblivion. At these extreme temperatures, once the cold gains ready access to the body, freezing comes almost in a flash. Lacking any protective clothing, the nude Rhea had, in effect, flash frozen, dead in moments, assuming she wasn't already dead when she was carried outside. I had no doubt that's what happened or who had done it.

"Does anyone know anything?" I asked. The gathered men shook their heads.

Bryan said, "No one here heard a sound. I'll talk to everyone else later."

"This one is self-evidently murder," I said.

"Yes, and we can take it that Rhea's was, as well."

The murmurs I heard said that this conclusion was a unanimous view. "We need to end this and return to Patriot Hills."

"I agree," Bryan said, "but Mr. Ainsworth won't do that. He's determined to make this climb, no matter what happens."

"You can call out and report what's going on, can't you?"

"Who would I report to? No nation has jurisdiction here. There's no police force, no courts. We might as well be on another planet." He touched my arm and pulled me away from the men as he was telling them to carry Ignacio to one of the supply shelters. When we were a distance away, he cut off his microphone and gestured for me to do the same, then we touched helmets. "My satellite phone is missing. Someone took it last night."

"Who?"

"I don't know. It might have been Pagan, but I don't think so. He never came near my stuff."

"One of your men, then."

"It must be. As for them being 'my men,' I didn't recruit them all. Some are allegedly on temporary duty from the Army. I have no way of knowing for certain. They don't all know each other, either. I've been taking them at face value so far, but I can't any longer. I can only trust those I recruited."

"Anyone else have a sat phone?"

"Just Ainsworth."

"So we're truly cut off."

"Completely." He said nothing for a long minute, then, "Let's get some sleep."

❧❧❧

That first 'day' at Camp Two, Bryan's team inspected each of the suits for signs of wear and proper functioning. So far they'd been subjected to little stress, as we'd spent most of our time outside the habitats within the ETVs, where the temperature placed no great strain on their designed capabilities. But on summit day they'd have to perform flawlessly under extreme conditions. That would be the major test of their durability.

Stern and Carlos had complained that their suits seemed given to extremes, first making them too hot, then too cold. For me and the rest of us, the suits had performed as advertised, but they were far more complicated than their simple functionality suggested. While it was true that the key was the layer of material that largely trapped our body's heat within them, making an artificial source of heat unnecessary, outside air had to be introduced and circulated. This was to maintain temperature and eliminate the inevitable build-up of humidity. This necessitated an access point between the safety of the interior and the deadly cold of the outside. Control of that access point was the difference between life and death for us. So far there'd been no significant problems.

Cold is the enemy of any battery, so the small pack that provided power to the helmet and where needed for the operation of the suit was contained within it, against my left side. It was small and generally unnoticed, though not entirely.

The helmets had also performed flawlessly. Only two of the men mentioned minor fogging, and one of Bryan's techs made an adjustment. Communication had worked as designed, which, in my military experience, was a first. It was always buggy when new and tended to get people killed.

Still, Bryan's team pored over the suits, running tests on the controls and batteries and checking for signs of wear. Zapata showed an interest in their work and followed them about, asking questions, remarking at how amazing the suits were. No one was happy to see him. He was told to go to bed repeatedly but refused, though he kept his distance.

The techs did not examine Ainsworth's suit or Pagan's. They were not allowed into that habitat, so Bryan saw to it.

Immediately after our suits were checked Stern and I donned them and went outside. We passed Zapata entering our habitat as we left. "Going for a stroll?" he asked.

"Taking some photos," Stern said, "if it's any of your business."

"Are you allowed?" I was thinking of the military gear with us.

"Why not?" he sniffed.

It was one thing to take photos, quite another to get them out of Antarctica, I thought.

We stepped through the double doors and into the night, where I stood for a moment, transfixed. I could never get over the beauty of our camps. The glowing, softly-colored habitats were luminescent, looking poised to lift gently into the black sky. Helmet beams and the banks of artificial lights cast brilliant and stark white slashes across the fresh, glittering snow.

Stern assumed a place on one of the adjacent hills and took a series of photos, including a bit of extended video. When he finished he gestured at his helmet, and I knew what he wanted. I reached over and killed his microphone as I did the same. Then we touched helmets.

"It's really started, hasn't it?" he said. "Bodies dropping left and right."

"I'm afraid so."

"You're snake bite, you know that? This happens every time I go on a climb with you. Listen, I'm reconsidering what you said yesterday. Maybe this isn't such a good idea for me, after all. I'm cut off out here, and we've got a killer running amok." He was silent for a moment then said, "Who is it, do you think?"

"I've got no evidence to suggest anyone."

Stern had a suspect in mind, for he said, "I can see him killing the girlfriend. I don't agree, you understand, she was something else, but couples kill one another all the time. But Ignacio? That makes no sense."

"How about Carlos?"

"Say, I didn't think of that. The Nazi angle, huh? And two killers. I like it. So Ignacio and his sister have it in for Carlos because he killed their brother, so Carlos takes one of them out. Let me think. If that's what this is, then Esmeralda needs to be very careful."

"I'd say so."

The response to Ignacio's murder over breakfast earlier had been as I'd expected. Everyone expressed shock and voiced a theory. I'd thought Ainsworth would have one of his meetings, but the task fell to Bryan instead. Esmeralda was in shock, he said, and remained in her habitat.

For the first time, one of Bryan's men spoke up. He stood up. "Sir, we've had two deaths and the expedition isn't even to the summit yet. What's being done about them?"

"Mr. Ainsworth is doing what he can, but as we all know, there are no legal authorities in Antarctica. I can assure you that this will all be reported to the Chilean police as soon as we return to Punta Arenas as that's the first place with government we'll touch.

United Nations protocols for Antarctica require that. I'm sure you can appreciate what has happened her is uncommon, very likely without precedent. Deaths in Antarctica are restricted to accidents or medical issues."

"Do you know if they've been advised by sat phone?"

"I do not. That is a decision for Mr. Ainsworth."

He sat down, then Zapata spoke. "What happened to Ignacio?"

"There's a tear in his suit, and that appears to be the reason he froze to death," Bryan answered.

"A tear? Or a cut?" Zapata persisted.

"It looked like a cut to me." Seeing the look of others, he added, "Yes, I agree, he was assaulted, and that resulted in his death."

"What are you doing about it?" Zapata demanded.

"What I can, which isn't much." Bryan straightened up and said, "Listen, we all need to face facts. No outsider came in here and killed Ignacio. He was murdered by someone on this expedition. Maybe the two of them got into a fight, and so this is self-defense or an accident. We don't know, but the fact that no one has stepped forward to say what took place tells a different story."

"Just what, exactly, is it you *are* doing?" Stern asked pointedly.

"We're gathering information on each event to present to the authorities once the climb is over. We're safeguarding the bodies for autopsy. What else can we do? Today is a rest day. My men will be conducting the equipment checks, so let them do their job. Just take it easy and stay out of each other's way."

"We should go back." This was Carlos. There were murmurs of agreement.

"At this point *we're* committed," Bryan said. "*You* are not. If any of you have changed your mind about attempting the summit you're welcome to remain here with the tech crew. Mr. Ainsworth has invested millions in this expedition. He's doing it in conjunction with the U.S. Department of Defense. You all know that the key equipment that makes this winter attempt possible is U.S. military in origin. The DOD is looking to our use of it under extreme conditions to help in its further development. So the climb will continue.

"As for the deaths, I can't account for them. I urge you all to remain in your habitats except when dining. If you must be outside, and I can think of no reason for that, then do so in pairs."

"The buddy system, huh?" one of the military types muttered. "Where have I heard that before."

"That's enough of that," Bryan snapped. "We all have a job to do, so let's see to it. The sooner Mr. Ainsworth and his team summit, the sooner we'll be back at Patriot Hills and out of here."

After a pause Zapata asked, "When will that be?"

"Tomorrow's another rest and a vehicle test day, summit the day after and return to Camp One, back to Patriot Hills the day after that. So it's three days from now."

"What's going on with the weather?" Kira asked, her voice sounding deadened.

"It's holding so far, but there's a pattern inland we're watching. It's stalled right now, but these fronts typically move onto the peninsula where we are. Like I say, we're keeping a close watch on it."

⌒⌒⌒

That had been earlier. Now when Stern finished with his photography and conversation we returned our habitat, then went to the dining hall. Bryan's crew was moving there for lunch, and I saw others coming, as well. Inside, it was steamy and warmer than the other habitats, as was always the case at mealtime. Again, neither Ainsworth nor Pagan made an appearance.

A very unhappy Esmeralda was seated at a table, and I sat across from her. I reached over and squeezed her hand. She looked up and gave me a wan smile just as the first plates of hot food came out.

Bryan rose. "I have a short announcement. In view of events the gathering tonight is canceled. I advise everyone to turn in early."

Zapata sat in a distant corner of the table, hunched over his meal, which I noticed he mostly stared at and pushed around on his plate. He coughed several times and drew unpleasant stares.

"Esmeralda," I said. "I know this is a difficult time for you, but what can you tell me about the Chilean Research Station? I've heard rumors."

"I don't know much." She looked exhausted. There were dark circles around her eyes. "I attended school with one of them and have met all the scientists over the last two years. It's under military authority now, but nothing much is different—except who they report to."

"Why military?"

She shrugged. "I only know rumors, probably the same ones you've heard. They don't talk about it. My friend says it was a funding issue."

"Some kind of discovery is what I was told."

"Yes, I've heard that one. Who can say?"

"The scientist who was flown back to Punta Arenas, was he dead or alive?"

She hesitated. "He died just before the departure."

Eleven

That night the wind awakened me. I heard it rushing down from the hills and scattering among the habitats. The triple layer of material between us and the outside made a peculiar fluttering sound, unlike any I'd heard before—not ominous, but disconcerting in that it suggested a fragility in the structure. When a strong gust struck the habitat, the facing wall quivered, and once I felt the structure sway under the force. It kept me awake for some time, but finally I drifted restlessly off.

I awakened to the sounds of activity and bright lights outside, as if a brilliant sun had arisen. A few moments later one of Bryan's men stuck his head in, his visor up, and shouted, "Mount up. Breakfast in ten minutes. Weather's coming this way and you're moving out first thing."

We scrambled to see to our needs and got to the dining habitat. An eager Ainsworth was waiting for everyone to arrive. He was jumpy, his bright, black eyes flashing in their intensity. When we were all seated he began. "As you've been told, this weather pattern we've been watching made its move a few hours ago and is coming directly at us. Once in motion such fronts tend to be predictable, I'm told. You likely felt the effects of the front last night as the wind picked up. I've decided to set out for the summit today. Those of you who wish to remain here are free to do so no matter what you've told me previously. Bryan and his men will hold the fort for us until we return. The plan had been for them to strike camp and move down to Camp One, where we'd join them later, but given the changing circumstances we'll plan to spend tonight here. We'll go directly to Patriot Hills in the morning. Weather permitting, the plane will arrive the next day and take us out."

"Who's making the attempt?" Stern asked.

"Esmeralda will lead, I will follow. We will, as planned, only use the single occupant ETVs, as they are slightly more maneuverable. The rest of you will follow. For now that is Scott, Quentin, Kira, and Carlos. Zapata is quite sick and will be remaining here. If any of you have changed your mind tell me now to spare us the effort of preparing for you. No one? All right, then enjoy your breakfast and eat your fill. With luck we'll be back in time for lunch, but you can never be certain about these things."

When I could I turned toward Stern and asked quietly, "Are you really going?"

"I think I'd better. Angel's not on the climbing team. That means he'll be here."

"What about you, Esmeralda? Are you up for this? You've got every right not to go. We'd understand."

She'd aged ten years overnight. "I want to. It will keep my mind off my brother, and the sooner we summit, the sooner I can get him home to our mother. I'll be all right. Anyway," she smiled weakly, "you need me to find the summit."

Kira and Carlos, I noticed, were in a heated discussion across the room. Carlos wanted something, but Kira wasn't giving. I could only guess at what that was about, but it was good to see them at odds.

Bryan came in with a rush of frigid air and removed his helmet. "We're about set. Suit up, then man your vehicles. Check everything three times. Be certain. One mistake is the only mistake you'll get. You're setting off as soon as you can."

Back in our habitat Stern and I climbed into our suits, double checking seals for each other and testing everything. "We look like space men," he said as we prepared to go outside. "I always wanted to be an astronaut."

Outside was windy, with occasional severe gusts. Sheets of loose snow kicked up and whipped across the camp. The ETVs were in a line, idling smoothly within their oversized tires, a vapor trail streaming from each, looking more like enormous insects than mechanical vehicles.

Esmeralda waved us over. "Kira will follow Señor Ainsworth once again, then Carlos, next Quentin, with you, Scott, bringing up the rear. Any questions? All right, let's load up."

I went to the last ETV, lifted the bubble, and climbed in. The temperature was already set for 35 degrees Fahrenheit. I scanned the instruments and found everything perfectly normal. There was a small container, set out of the way on the floor, and I checked it. Water, nutrition bars, first aid kit, all in case we were out longer than we planned. I hoped I wouldn't need any of it. I plugged the suit into the power supply.

I was ready to go, but instead we sat unmoving as the engine idled. After ten minutes there was a knock on the bubble. I popped it open. It was Bryan. He reached over, killed my microphone, then touched helmets with me. "Need anything?"

"What's going on with the storm?"

"It's not due until very late today. You should be fine, and we'll be here to lend a hand if necessary."

"What's the delay about?"

"We can't find Carlos."

And they didn't find him, even after a systematic search. The climbers were told to stay inside the vehicles. Finally, Ainsworth came on the radio with an announcement. "We have no idea where Carlos is, but we're going now. We're wasting fuel and our weather window. Angel is taking his place. Follow instructions and you'll all be fine."

I waited to see if Stern was going to bail, but he didn't. People, I'd observed, are like that. Once they've made a decision, then gone to the trouble of setting it in motion, they tend not to turn away from it—even when the situation has changed.

I tried to make heads or tails out of it but could not. It was simply a strange development. Pagan coming along made no climbing sense at all. Just then the ETVs ahead began moving like an accordion and I followed. Esmeralda took it easy for the first few miles, holding our speed to a cautious crawl. Today was when the ETVs were have to been checked and serviced I recalled. But that hadn't taken place. Still, they'd not been subjected to much strain getting from Patriot Hills to Camp Two.

Our route rose slowly, wandering between small hills and around rugged terrain. We stopped frequently, and more than once Esmeralda climbed out of her ETV to walk ahead and check the way. We took several detours, which slowed our progress even more.

The wind buffeted my ETV continuously though not violently. Our headlights pierced the darkness, which appeared even blacker than usual. Sheets of snow that had lifted from the surface flashed across our way, giving the little caravan a ghostly aspect. Once, as we made a slow turn to avoid an enormous crevice and I caught sight of the other vehicles, I was reminded of an enormous centipede.

Esmeralda slowly increased our speed, but we still crawled safely across even, non-threatening terrain. In retrospect, her caution should not have come as a surprise. Summit day is the most dangerous of any expedition. Most leaders practice an excess of care in that final approach. That was what Esmeralda was doing.

Because we could not talk to one another there was no idle chatter, and she was all business when she did speak. I didn't hear from Ainsworth again.

Sitting at idle or traveling across the occasional unchallenging terrain, I had plenty of time to consider what Stern had told me. Every climb I'd made during these last few years had been deadly. In part I understood that was because I'd been sent by the DIA, so an element of danger was to be expected. But there was more to it than that. The climb on Mt. McKinley had been nothing but murder and accidental deaths—shockingly so—and I'd been on vacation.[4] I was starting to think that Stern had a point and that either I should give up expedition climbs or stop climbing altogether.

Rhea was dead, murdered all but certainly. Ignacio had been killed, and now Carlos was missing. It was unlikely he was within

---

4   See *Murder on Mt. McKinley*.

the camp itself after such a thorough search, so that meant he was away from it. Perhaps he was just out there for some reason known only to him. Perhaps he was out there—but dead.

It occurred to me that he might have stayed behind to search for the idols. I'd seen Kira climb into her ETV, and she'd not had them with her. Did she trust him enough to know where they were? How could she keep them away from him in these close conditions? But if she had, that might very well be what they'd been arguing over, and he'd elected to stay behind and find the things. She'd decided to stick close to Ainsworth, as he was her ticket to a future, and Carlos wasn't going anywhere with them even if he did find them. But if that was the case, she couldn't have liked it.

Most significantly, Pagan had taken his place. That could very well be the real reason Carlos was suddenly unavailable. If Stern was to die on this climb, this struck me as a very good time to do it.

We began to climb more steeply, but the weather held, getting no worse. As I recalled, Vinson Massif was the highest spine on a mountain ridge. At some point we'd come to a place even the ETVs couldn't manage, and so we'd have to stop. From there we'd make the assault on foot.

An hour into the drive, Esmeralda said, "I'm slowing now. We'll pull into a semi-circle here and park. Leave your ETVs running, as instructed. If you turn them off we'll never get them fired up again in these temperatures."

She had a point. Between the storm and higher elevation, the outside temperature was minus 71 degrees.

We slowed, then ahead I saw the first vehicle swing wide to the left. Ainsworth, Kira, Pagan, Stern and I followed. We came to rest in a sort of fishhook.

"Take a drink now," Esmeralda said. "It will be our last until we get back. "

I took her advice and had a long pull of water; it tasted like plastic. Then I lowered my visor and lifted the bubble. I stepped outside and closed the bubble, careful to make certain it sealed properly.

At this greater elevation the wind was much stronger, and for a long minute I was chilly before the suit did its magic and I was comfortable again. Once everyone else was out I worked my way along the ETV, confirming that each one was running, then joined the gathering in front.

Esmeralda called us over. "We're further down than I wanted. Conditions are much rougher than they were five months ago, when I was last here. We've got a stiff climb ahead of us. There's plenty of snow where I've not seen any previously, and I'm afraid the going may be tough. Stick with the line and don't drop back. I'll set a reasonable pace. If anyone has a problem, just call out."

Despite her concern, I was beginning to accept that we'd be able to do this even in these arctic conditions. Lacking the usual backpack, since anything I'd need would be frozen into uselessness, and given the relatively light weight and comfort of the suit, this was the most at ease I'd ever been on summit day. We'd not left at midnight, as was typical, following a miserable night in a high bivouac, frozen to our bones even before we'd left our tent, chipping our boots out of ice, eating snow to prevent dehydration, cooking porridge over an altitude-starved flame with numb fingers. Instead, I'd had a comfortable night's sleep, then ridden in a Mars-style vehicle to within striking distance of the summit.

"All right," Esmeralda said. "Everyone can hear everyone now. Please don't talk and tie up the communication system. Let's go." With that, we set out.

Though Vinson Massif is along a ridge that would typically expose us to the brutal elements, the back side of the spine was a flowing mound of undulating snow. It rose more sharply than any ground we'd covered until now—but was still a modest rise. The spine to our right served to shield us from the worst of the wind.

We moved in a line, with Esmeralda leading the way, carrying a bright handheld light that she brandished before us. Ainsworth followed her, then Stern, Pagan, Kira, and me. We'd not been exercising the right muscles for some days, and Esmeralda wisely took it easy, stopping every few minutes to settle us into the pace. The suits might keep us from freezing, but the human body still had to cover the distance.

We soon encountered heavy drifts. Esmeralda forced a path through them and we followed. They slowed us considerably. In more common summit conditions, this slowdown would not have troubled me, but I was concerned about how much of this the suits could take. As they were military in origin I assumed they'd hold up, but assumptions get you killed—and I'd seen more than one bit of military hardware break apart while doing exactly what it was designed for.

I could do nothing about my suit however. My greatest concern was the weather as the temperature was falling below the margin Ainsworth had anticipated. Every degree below zero is significant, but once the temperature falls below minus 50 degrees, life becomes very uncertain. Seventy below was unacceptable anywhere in the world—except for the shortest of durations, and then only with every inch of skin covered and with the rest of you bundled in the extreme. Any mistake now, any malfunction of our suits, and we'd be frozen within a few short minutes. Fully exposed, we wouldn't last more than a few seconds.

Then there was the approaching storm. I hadn't had much luck with such fronts in recent climbs. They always seemed to make the most deadly move just when you needed a break. It was my hope that we'd not see this storm until after we were safely back in Camp Two but I wasn't counting on it.

For now, though, the climbing was not difficult. Despite that, Ainsworth was in awe of the experience. You'd have thought he was Hillary about to summit Everest for the first time. "My God," he said repeatedly. "I can't get over this. Just look. It's amazing!"

Actually, there was almost nothing to see other than the splashing light from our helmets and the wall of night surrounding us. At dawn on most summit days you were well into the climb, having left in the middle of the night. The view was spectacular, often breathtaking in its naked beauty. You were on the highest peak in the region, and the earth seemed to melt away from you in a succession of lesser mountains. The air at altitude is sparkling clear and so close to the sun piercing a thinner atmosphere that the colors are more vivid, the greys of rock more stark. Photographs simply don't do such vistas justice.

Here, there was nothing but an endless, Cimmerian night, broken only by the beams of our helmets and Esmeralda's bright light, which lit the area before her like a floodlight. But Ainsworth was in ecstasy. I couldn't help but sense some of what he said was an act, forced, as if it was expected of him.

Contrary to all my concerns, the suit continued to function properly, adjusting itself to my exertions. Even my feet, normally unfeeling at this point, were vital and warm.

The only unusual moment occurred at the one truly dangerous place along this route. We passed a narrow precipice, not as daunting as many I'd encountered over the years though in this darkness each climber had to be very careful of his footing. Esmeralda warned us as we approached it. The line slowed and proceeded cautiously. Then I saw Stern suddenly stumble and cry out. For a crazy instant his arms flayed about like a windmill, then, as abruptly as it started, he was away from the edge and safely to the other side. It was the only close call.

After that there were more snow mounds. Esmeralda continued leading the way through them. I didn't know the exact number, but she'd accomplished this climb more than a dozen times before. On other expeditions, this was work reserved for the local guides, as it was exhausting. Lacking them in some instances, every climber usually would take a turn on point. I suggested it twice, but both times she told me it was no problem. I knew better, but for some reason she wanted to reserve this for herself.

Still we made steady, if uneven, progress up the mountain, and no one complained of a problem—surprisingly, not even Stern. We stopped often enough and rested while Esmeralda cleared a path, and in between those pauses she set a modest pace.

So it was that 97 minutes after leaving the ETVs we were at the summit. The last 100 yards were a series of zigzags as we rose sharply. Breaking free of the protective wall of the spine the wind increased in volume. Esmeralda announced the peak as we neared. Ainsworth said nothing as he moved before her so he'd be the first

on top, as if no one had ever been there before. Each of us followed in line until we joined him.

As is the case with so many summits, we stood atop a round embankment of snow. Hillary, I'd read, had been initially reluctant to go to the very peak of Everest because it appeared to him it was a bank overhanging a precipice. So it was here. But there was a large area just below it for us to cluster on, and we six stood there a few moments in exultation. It is our nature to want to stand on high ground, and the highest ground always filled me with an emotion that defies adequate description.

As nothing inhibited it, the wind was very strong on the peak, and I could feel it pressing hard against me. My suit was busy adjusting itself to this new state. The night that enveloped us was unrelenting, severely limiting the short distance I could see in any direction. I tried to catch a glimpse of Camp Two, which should have been a beacon in the near distance, but saw nothing. I'd expected a glow against the sky—something. But all I saw was the endless stretch of night.

Ainsworth was, of course, eager for photographs, and Esmeralda saw to them. She took a series of the conqueror alone, visor up, visor down, followed by more with him brandishing various corporate flags bearing logos.

After that he insisted I join him for another series, visors up, visors down. Finally, he had me take his photo with Esmeralda. She looked exhausted, which caught me by surprise. Clearing our route had apparently been even more taxing than I'd thought. Neither Stern nor Kira had their pictures taken, though Kira suggested it, nor, for that matter did Pagan, who had yet to say a word.

Now, for the first time, my suit malfunctioned. The temperature suddenly plummeted within it. It was as if it had ceased functioning. I was at once freezing and began to shake violently. I slapped at my side where the air entry point was located, but nothing changed. My teeth began to chatter.

I thought how far I was from the ETV, asking myself whether, if I ran, it would keep my body temperature up long enough to make it to one of the heated vehicles before freezing to death. But a second thought told me that I could not. It was simply too far.

Then, with no visible change I could detect, the suit suddenly reheated, and I was soon bathed in warmth. My panic subsided, but any level of trust I'd previously had for the suit was absolutely gone.

"Anyone having trouble with his suit?" I asked. "Stern?"

"No. It's been okay."

"What happened?" Esmeralda asked.

"I was suddenly very, very cold, but it's all right now. I just wondered if anyone else was experiencing the same problem." No one had.

In the minutes before we formed up to leave, Stern joined me but said nothing and just stayed close to my side. Esmeralda announced it was time to descend. Despite our longer than anticipated climb, it was early yet. We were not three hours out from Camp Two, and at this pace we would return in time for a late lunch. I was thinking this when I heard a cough.

"Who was that?" Esmeralda asked.

Kira raised a hand. "It's nothing. I just swallowed wrong."

"Let's head back, if that's all right with you," Esmeralda said. There was no reason to say who "you" was.

"Yes, I must say, it has been a fantastic experience." It was Ainsworth's voice. "I can see why you love this so, Scott. It is invigorating. Still, I must admit it's a bit disappointing. It's been too easy."

"We aren't home yet," I said.

Esmeralda assumed the lead, followed by Ainsworth, and then came Pagan and Kira. Stern hung back, taking his place behind his ex-wife, with me bringing up the rear.

I glanced at the exterior temperature. I was shocked: minus 107 degrees. A moment later Esmeralda fired up her heavy-duty light and set out back the way we'd come. Each of us took our place in line. Someone coughed again, but no one asked this time who it was.

Twelve

Going down is less effort than going up, though not always easier and often more treacherous. In this case, with the spine of the mountain ridge shielding us from the increasingly violent wind and the relatively benign slope of the descent, it was without major difficulty. Our pathway through the snow mounds was already cleared, and no significant new snow had fallen along our route while we were on the summit.

There were few words, though there were more coughs. I wondered if the air within the suits was too dry, or if somehow we'd caught the bug the scientists had brought to Patriot Hills. The time frame seemed too fast to me, but I was no expert.

Just under one hour after we set out we approached the ETVs. Esmeralda flashed her powerful light towards them from some distance, and there they were, in fish hook formation, looking as inviting as a summer beach. Ten minutes later we arrived and saw a startling reality.

The ETVs sat frozen in place, already glazed over with a sheet of ice. None of the engines were running.

Esmeralda shone her light on her lead vehicle. It looked to me as if it had been carved from a block of ice. She tried to open the bubble. It was frozen shut. So there was a second design flaw. The engineers should have anticipated that at some point the ETVs would be caught in extreme cold and would therefore have provided a failsafe way to open them up. Of course, it might have made no difference. Any temperature severe enough to seal the bubble that fast had done the same to the engine.

The first flaw, of course, was building a vehicle that couldn't maintain an idle in these conditions. That should have been basic.

I moved to the second ETV and found it the same. Stern walked along them, trying each bubble in turn, unable to open any of the vehicles.

"What's going on?" Ainsworth snapped, though it was obvious to everyone except him.

"The ETVs stopped running while we were gone," Esmeralda said. "They're frozen solid."

"That's impossible. They're designed for these conditions. I've seen the reports." He sounded as if he was trying to convince himself.

"Lab conditions are not the same as those in the field," I said. "In case you haven't noticed, it's more than 100 degrees below zero, and the wind chill factor makes it even worse."

"I…I was assured that this couldn't happen," he persisted. "If I'd known about it, I would never have made this expedition."

"What are we going to do?" That was Kira, sounding a little hysterical. "I don't want to die!"

"No one's going to die," Esmeralda snapped. "Everyone just calm down."

"You bitch," Ainsworth snarled. "You should have a backup plan. Why are we stranded up here with no help? Why didn't you leave someone to make certain the ETVs kept running?"

"I suggested it, and you said it was unnecessary and a waste of manpower. I urged you to change your mind just after breakfast today. Remember?"

"Don't take that tone with me!" Ainsworth shouted. "If you thought it important, you should have insisted, not left us to die up here with no hope of rescue!"

"Let's all calm down and stop the name-calling. What's done is done. What we need is a plan," I said. "Esmeralda, what's the next step?"

But before she could answer, Ainsworth barked, "Pagan, break into that thing. Let's get at least one going." No one needed to ask who would ride out in it.

Pagan had no tools to break into anything, but he approached Ainsworth's ETV and worked on the bubble for some minutes, moving it back and forth, trying to pry it open, all without success.

"We can't get the bubbles open," I said, after it was obvious— even to Ainsworth. "Bryan warned me about this. At these temperatures, they must keep operating to stay warm. We have no way to get any of them running even if you could get the bubble open."

"What are we going to do?" Ainsworth asked, his voice rising in pitch. Pagan stopped wasting his time on the bubble.

"Oh, God," Kira said and fell back in the snow. "Oh, God. I can't believe this is happening. Why me? What am I doing here?"

"Come on," Stern said reaching down for her. "Get up. You shouldn't be in the snow like that."

"What do you know about it?" Kira snarled. "If it wasn't for you, I wouldn't even be here. You've ruined everything. You've destroyed my life."

"We can't possibly walk back!" Ainsworth whined. "I just know we can't."

"Of course we can," Esmeralda said. "That's always been the backup plan. It's not far."

"How many miles is it?" Kira asked, sitting up. Stern reached down for her again and she slapped his hand away.

"About ten. I'd say three to four hours, since we'll be going downhill. The wind may slow us a bit. And that assumes the weather doesn't get any worse."

"Or our suits don't malfunction. Scott's already reported a problem with his. Can't you call out for the tandem ETVs to pick us up?" Stern asked. "They're safe and snug inside a warm shelter."

There was a pause, then Ainsworth answered. "Not unless we can get into my ETV. I left the sat phone, since it would freeze at these temperatures. Perhaps you men can find a way to force it open even though Pagan couldn't."

"It's pointless," I said. "First, these are designed to military specifications. We'd need the right tools to force one open. Second, your sat phone is frozen solid already and useless to us."

"We need to get going," Esmeralda said. "The storm is coming, and while we have enough time to return to Camp Two sometimes storms move faster than predicted. We don't want to take any chances."

Ainsworth wanted to argue about it, and we lost precious minutes as she persuaded him there would be no miracles. The only way out was on foot, and the sooner we left, the better. Finally, he saw the logic of it and consented.

"Get up, Kira," Stern said. "If you stay there you'll die. Come on. We're walking back to Camp Two."

Again she slapped away his proffered hand. As she got her feet she said, "You're a condescending SOB, you know that, Quentin? You deserve everything that's going to happen to you."

Esmeralda led the way again, as she knew it, which was a good thing. The billowing snow blown across our route up meant that our tracks were already partially covered. It wouldn't be long before we'd have no path to follow. But she'd done this many times before, and even without a marked route I was certain she could find the way back.

I was starting to get thirsty. No one wasted energy on complaining.

Only the wind made the going a struggle. The existing snow was flat and reasonably firm. My boots sank no more than three inches into it. The suit kept me comfortable, though I no longer had confidence in it. Any second I expected it to malfunction and plunge me into freezing temperatures. I knew it could fail, that it would fail. I just didn't know when.

This was the way with technology. I'd seen it time and again, both in the military and on various expeditions. Someone introduced a new gadget guaranteed to work like a wonder, to make life easier and safer, and when you most needed it the gadget failed. Well, DOD got what they wanted out of this. They'd just learned that their wonder toys couldn't keep an idle below 100 degrees, and for a vehicle that had to keep running to stay operational that was a problem.

Then another thought crept into my mind. What if they'd been sabotaged?

⌒⌒⌒

The wind maintained its intensity and billowing gusts of snow swept over us with regularity. Slowly the trail our ETVs had left behind vanished, to be replaced only by the footsteps of those trudging ahead of me.

The temperature was holding at minus 97 degrees, give or take a degree or two. I didn't want to dwell on the thought of sabotage, but my mind returned to it repeatedly. Bryan had expressed concern about the loyalty of one of his men, but it could have been anyone not on the summit attempt. Since Ainsworth was with us, it was no one loyal to him, but I couldn't help wonder just who *was* loyal to him. He was a man with many enemies. If, as Bryan suspected, someone on his team had turned traitor, then why couldn't the same be true of those Ainsworth thought he'd paid off?

This was an ideal place for murder, as were each of the Seven Summits. There are so many different ways to die in the conditions necessary to climb them. I'd certainly seen enough of it over recent years. This expedition had been common knowledge in certain circles for some months, commonly known beyond that in the more recent weeks. A winter assault of Vinson Massif was, by definition, a deadly undertaking. One as dependent on technology as this one provided many opportunities for sabotage. Ainsworth was certain to be on the team that tried to summit. What better time to tamper with the equipment?

But did it stop with the ETVs? We could be expected to hike back to Camp Two if they were disabled. Had the same saboteur done something to our suits? Was that why I was having trouble with it?

If he had, we were all dead.

After two hours the weather took a turn for the worse. I looked at the temperature and read minus 95 degrees. I felt no different within my suit except that I was now very thirsty. I'd made a decision not to lift my visor to eat snow, as getting enough fluid that way was time consuming and I didn't want to do it very often. Releasing all that warmth from within meant the system had to work harder to maintain my body temperature, and I didn't want to risk that. I could afford to be thirsty a while longer.

The wind was stronger now, gusting, I estimated, to 50 miles an hour. Snow was no longer blocked by the terrain as we'd cleared the protective spine and whipped across our pathway continuously.

There was more coughing, enough to cause concern. I told myself it was the dry air, though my readout claimed humidity was a steady 45%. I didn't want to consider what else the coughs suggested. Coughing was catchy, like a yawn, and signified nothing. I had plenty of the tangible to worry about without adding even more speculation.

Three hours out from the ETVs Esmeralda called a halt. We gathered in the partial shelter of a modest, snow covered hill. Like sheep in a blizzard, we clustered together.

"How is everyone?" she asked, sounding very tired herself. Occasionally a glimmer of light lit a face, but it was only for a second, and the images weren't always reassuring. Fighting the wind and dispirited from the failure of our equipment, we were a depressed, weary group.

There were general comments of assurance all around, then Esmeralda said, "We should reach Camp Two any time now. We're all tired, so I'm not going to push our pace. Just keep together."

When we set out again the wind eased and there was much less billowing snow. We'd done it, though I'd never really doubted we would, absent a serious equipment failure. This was not that great a distance to go, and as long as the suits continued to function as designed I'd seen no reason why we couldn't make it to Camp Two. With the considerable resources there, I anticipated no problem making our way to Base Camp.

Twenty minutes later Esmeralda came to a stop. I looked ahead and saw nothing other than what I'd been seeing for the last three hours. There were no lights, no glowing habitats, nothing to suggest Camp Two.

"We're here," she said.

"What do you mean 'we're here'?" Ainsworth demanded. "There's *nothing* here. You must have lost your way."

"This is the location for Camp Two," she said, sounding shocked.

"Where are they?" Stern said. "Where is everybody? Did they pack up and leave us? I can't believe it!"

"We need to spread out and conduct a search," Esmeralda said.

"What are you talking about?" Kira said, almost hysterically. "There's no camp. There's no one! There's nothing here but snow. There's nothing to search for!"

Esmeralda again ordered us to line up and then to walk across the area where she insisted Camp Two was located. I was certain she had the wrong spot—or perhaps I hoped she had, as the implications were staggering if this was, indeed, the place. In the end, we all did as we were told.

Thirty feet ahead we discovered the remains of a habitat, collapsed on itself. The beds within, tables and chairs, all gave it a lumpy appearance, as did the exterior fuel cell, but it was all subdued by a layer of snow and ice. It was a habitat; dead as only an inanimate object could be.

"Check for survivors," Esmeralda ordered. But her voice said it all.

Thirteen

There were, of course, no survivors.

What had once been Camp Two just a few short hours before was now a windswept desolation, as utterly frozen as the vast continent about us. All apparent signs of the camp had vanished and was remained would not have been recognizable as a place of habitation by man if we'd not known it to be one.

Within the habitats we found most of the support team. Many of them had been in their long johns when the habitats integrity had been ruptured. Some had tried to get into their suits, but the ceiling had collapsed on them almost at once, and it had been hopeless. They'd died within a few short minutes.

We found a body outside in his suit. It had been sliced open like Ignacio's, but in this case there was no doubt that there had been a very violent struggle, as there were many cuts and gashes. Dark patches I took to be frozen blood lined each rupture. It was Bryan.

We worked out way meticulously across the camp a second then a third time in vain hope of finding someone alive but it was hopeless. The wind was picking up, a reminder that the storm was not far behind. The worst news was that the shelter containing the remaining ETVs had likewise been ruptured and the vehicles were frozen into blocks of ice.

Given conditions with the storm, the covering of ice and snow across everything, and the difficulty of gaining access to each habitat, we finally ceased our rescue efforts. This was work for a body recovery team.

At one point I spotted Pagan meeting alone with Ainsworth, their helmets touching in private conversation. I'd like to have been a fly on the wall. Not long thereafter we gathered to consider what to do. After more expressions of shock, fear and speculation about what had happened and who had done it, Ainsworth spoke. "One of the tandem ETVs is missing. Whoever did this is on his way to Patriot Hills to escape, leaving us to die." He sounded a bit hysterical.

And whoever that was had killed everyone else and tried to kill us—though, admittedly, the verdict on that was still out.

"We should check all the bodies and learn who it is," Pagan said.

"There's no time for that," I answered. "And we don't know how many were outside in suits. It could take hours, even days, to find everybody—and even then we couldn't be certain."

"Maybe someone got away," Kira suggested.

"It's possible," I allowed. "But if they were in the area they'd be looking for us and should have come back by now."

"I don't think a survivor of a massacre like this would stick around," Stern said. "I sure wouldn't."

"If a survivor set out for Patriot Hills alone on foot, could he make it?" I asked Esmeralda.

She hesitated, then said, "I doubt it. He wouldn't know the route, for one thing. Even if he knew the direction to head originally it would be very easy to lose his way, especially in these conditions. No, anyone out there alone on foot hasn't got a chance."

"How about the man or men in the ETV?" I asked. "Can he make it?"

"Maybe. He certainly has a better chance, but knowing the route and sticking to it will be difficult."

"He'll have GPS," I said.

"Yes, there's that. But with the storm it isn't as easy as just seeing the point where you are going."

"What do we do now?" Stern asked. "Are you certain you can't get the ETVs to run?"

I'd checked. "They're dead. I wish we could fire them up, but it's hopeless. There's only one way out of here. How far is it to Patriot Hills?" I asked.

"It's 53 miles," Esmeralda answered. "We can do it."

"Fifty-three miles!" The voice was Kira's. "We just walked 20. In these conditions, it's hopeless!"

"We've only come ten miles," Esmeralda said. "Fifty-three will be difficult, I admit, but it is manageable. It's our only option. We have to keep moving. Bad as it is now, the storm is heading towards us and it will get much worse yet."

"Maybe there's some gear here we could use. I'm really thirsty and hungry." That was Kira again. "Maybe we can get one of the habitats back up and heated. Then find some way to call for help."

"Everything's frozen solid," I said. "There's nothing of use to us here any longer. You might try eating snow, but to get enough you'll have to open your visor repeatedly, and I don't know if putting your suit through the strain is worth the risk."

"But I'm really thirsty."

"My God," I heard Ainsworth whine, "why would someone do this to me? What did I ever do to deserve this?"

"Let's go," Esmeralda said with resignation as she turned and headed out. Reluctantly it seemed, the rest followed.

I gave us less than one chance in five of making it. First, we were completely dependent on Esmeralda, as only she knew the route and she was pretty beat already. There would be no food, no water for the 16 to 20 hours I estimated this would take. Second, the storm might make it impossible to continue, either because she would be unable to find the route or because the conditions would be too extreme. Finally, we couldn't be certain how long these suits would function in these conditions.

The outside temperature had fallen to minus 97 degrees. In even lower temperatures and over time I was all but certain our suits would fail. In addition, it would only take a single wear spot or puncture to violate their integrity and make an ice block out of the wearer.

No, we stood very little chance.

Rescue was a non-starter. We were cut off from communication with Patriot Hills already, and that should have alerted the two-man team there. But they had no resources to mount a rescue. They were there to keep the camp operational. It was possible they'd send out word, but by the time anyone responded it would be too late. And Antarctica in the dead of winter would require the kind of specialized equipment we'd come with to be of any help to us. No, rescue was out of the question. We were on our own.

It wouldn't be possible to hike another 53 miles without fluids, so against my own argument I began reaching down and scooped up a handful of snow every once in a while. Traditionally, this is a practice all mountaineers condemn, as the amount of water you actually get from that little snow is meager, and the cold has a tendency to lower your core body temperature, a dangerous condition.

With the suits, I wasn't concerned about that, and if I'd been more comfortable with the ability of the suit I'd have satisfied myself with snow. As it was, I did it only intermittently. All the rest, I saw, had also taken to the practice.

Esmeralda hiked for an hour, then took a five minute break, military style. No one had much to say except for Ainsworth, who complained at the first three stops. After that he was too tired.

Our route was not especially demanding. If it had been, we'd have had no chance at all. But there were rugged spots that Esmeralda led us through. We'd skirted these with the ETVs on the outbound leg, but now she wanted to keep the distance as short as possible. For all her bravado, hiking another 50 miles after the day we'd already put in was asking a great deal. We were only attempting it because we had no choice.

The rough patches consisted of projecting ice covered with a new layer of snow. We made our way through these fields awkwardly, but they required no special tools and presented no extraordinary difficulty. Kira complained, as did Ainsworth, but the rest of us just gutted them out. No one was thinking about the idols any longer.

As is often the case on climbs it was a question of putting one foot in front of the other, turning the mind off, just moving your feet. I concentrated on that and nothing else as long as I could.

The first to die was Pagan. He complained during our fifth hour out that he was cold. Having been there, I sympathized. It was my worst fear. We stopped and systematically checked his suit, working our way slowly from his helmet to his boots. Kira spotted a tear near his left ankle. We had nothing with which to patch it. We could only hope the suit's capacity could overcome the leak.

It did not.

Pagan continued to complain of cold as we proceeded. Then we could hear his teeth chattering. Finally, he stopped. He stood a bit, then sat in the snow. We gathered about him. Pagan slumped forward between his knees.

"Let's go," Ainsworth said after a minute. "There's nothing we can do for him."

Pagan said something softly in Spanish. "What was that?" Kira asked.

"He's talking to his mother," Esmeralda said, lifelessly.

"Let's go," Ainsworth repeated. "I don't want to see this." He bent down and patted Pagan on the back. "I'll take care of your family, Angel. You can trust me." Then he turned and walked off. "Come on. He's as good as dead."

Coldhearted as it was, he was right, and there was nothing we could do. Reluctantly we set out, the five of us. I checked the time. It was just after 8:00 pm. Half an hour later the coughing began in earnest.

Even though I was all but certain we were going to die, I've been on worse treks. Both times I'd descended from Everest in conditions worse than this, in a far more perilous and hopeless state than I was now. My summer descent from Aconcagua had been much more touch and go than this, so far, as it took place in the midst of a blizzard. But the failure of Pagan's suit confirmed what I feared—that they weren't really up to the stress of such a long march in difficult conditions. And there was more than one way for them to fail.

Over the next hour I realized that we were slowly losing our headlamps. I'd never asked how long they could operate but was now seeing the reality. If we lost all light in these conditions, we'd be helpless.

Not that I could tell how Esmeralda was managing to keep us on course. She'd trekked this route many times, and I took from that she knew what markers to look for. In the pitch black that surrounded us, I was amazed it was possible. From time to time she flashed her brilliant light left, then right, as if taking her bearings, and I never once saw her hesitate.

When next we stopped, our helmet lights had grown quite feeble. "Perhaps we should turn our lights off," I suggested. "At this rate we'll be in the dark anyway. Better to preserve even some light for an emergency."

"We can't do that!" It was Ainsworth "We'd stumble around and get lost!"

"We'd stay in line and follow Esmeralda. How long is your handheld light good for?" I asked.

"Up to 30 hours, but this cold will likely cut its life. I agree with Scott. You all should turn off your lights. I should have thought of that sooner."

This time the rest stop lasted nearly ten minutes. There was little talk after that but quite a bit of coughing and hacking from Kira, Ainsworth, and even Esmeralda. So far, Stern and I weren't joining in.

"All right," Esmeralda said. "Stay close to the climber in front of you and keep your eyes on where my light shines. You'll be fine."

Though Ainsworth was immediately behind her, he refused to kill his light as the rest of us did.

I was getting very tired by this time. I'd been continuously on my feet since we left the ETVs that morning for the summit. Because of the constant night there was a tendency to think that time stood still, but, in fact, we'd already put in a long, exhausting day and could expect much more to come. We were moving generally downhill and no climbing was required of us, but moving through the wind and maintaining a steady pace was slowly draining me of energy. I was now hungry as well as thirsty.

There was a frightening minute when my suit failed again. I was suddenly very cold. I said nothing to the others. What was there to say? Was it a tear, like with Pagan? Had the regulator malfunctioned again? I had no way of knowing. I kept walking and resolved to keep going as long as I could.

Then, as my teeth began to chatter, the suit righted itself and I was again bathed in warmth. I pressed the experience out of my thoughts. I had no control over the suit. What would happen would happen. Unable to turn my mind off, I revisited events.

So what had happened at Camp Two? Someone, or perhaps two someones—since a tandem ETV had been taken—had killed everyone. With the exception of Bryan, whoever it was pulled it off by stripping them of heat and exposing them to the elements. In these extreme temperatures, nature had very quickly done the job for him.

Who?

Had it been possible to identify all the bodies, I would have known by the process of elimination. Perhaps it was one of Bryan's men, as he'd suspected, though it could just as easily have been Zapata. He could have faked being ill to remain behind while Kira tackled the summit without the idols. He'd killed Carlos, then—once we'd set out—he'd found the idols. After that he killed everyone and left us to die. He'd reach Patriot Hills alone, with the idols, tell a story that covered what others would later discover, then leave with the plane. He'd take the idols to his hero, Hugo Chavez, and reap his reward.

But it could just as easily have been Carlos. Feeling he was being betrayed, untrusting of Kira, who was getting too cozy with Ainsworth, he'd hid out until we left for the summit. Then he'd found the idols and killed everyone. For this to work meant he'd given up on the possibility of selling them to Ainsworth and was confident he could find a buyer on his own.

There was no way for me to know. It might just as easily have been someone else, and the idols may have had nothing to do with it. They were buried somewhere in Camp Two. They'd be covered every year with a fresh layer of snow and vanish from existence.

One of Ainsworth's enemies could very well have set this up to get rid of him. Perhaps the real objective was either to discredit the high tech gear we were using or to destroy whoever in Washington supported it.

The possibilities were limitless, but they filled my idle thoughts as I stayed in line and pushed from my mind the inevitability of my impending death.

The wind increased in intensity, though the temperature fell no further. Until now the snow had been largely that lifted from the surface by the wind, but now a fresh snowfall was intermixed, cutting our visibility even more.

It became self-evident that Esmeralda, Ainsworth and Kira were genuinely sick. When we stopped, after three hours, they each coughed almost continuously, Esmeralda even bending at the waist, bracing herself with her elbows to her knees as she hacked.

"How do you feel?" I asked them, in general, my communication set broadcasting to everyone.

Kira answered first. "I'm really hot. I think I've got a fever. I need to rest. Can't we build a shelter or something and wait this storm out?"

"We need to keep moving," Esmeralda said, straightening up. "If we stop for an extended time we'll be lying in our graves."

"I don't think I can keep this up much longer," Ainsworth said. "I'm really sick." He suddenly snapped his visor open, bent over and threw up, dropping to his knees and dry heaving for more than a very long minute.

Kira emitted a plaintive sound then collapsed into the snow, as if that was the last straw for her.

I looked hard at Esmeralda, who seemed to waver on her feet. When Ainsworth finally stopped, still kneeling as he gasped for air, she said, "Get up. Both of you. We aren't waiting, and if you stay behind you are dead. We still have a long way to go and have to keep moving."

I reached down and helped Ainsworth to his feet. As he slowly reached up to close his visor my eyes followed his hand and I was shocked by what I saw. His face was pockmarked with vivid blisters, his lips were cracked and bleeding, his eyes glazed over. He looked like the victim of a plague from the Middle Ages. I moved away from him.

Stern, to my surprise, silently raised Kira to her feet. She did nothing to resist him. Esmeralda said nothing more. Instead, she turned from us and, flashing the light before her, set off toward Patriot Hills.

Ten minutes later we came on the tandem ETV.

Fourteen

The vehicle sat frozen in place. Two feet of snow was piled against one side, emphasizing its abandonment. The bubble was glazed over and impossible to open. I rubbed at the surface, turned on my light, then peered in. It was empty.

"How long do you think it's been here?" Stern asked, standing beside me.

"I can't say. Once it stopped working it would have frozen solid within minutes. It might only have been here a half hour, or several hours. There's no telling."

"Any sign of who it was?"

"No. Nothing."

The others were sheltered against the ETV's side, leaning up against it for support. Ainsworth's light had dimmed to near extinction. From what I'd seen of him, it didn't matter.

"Where do you think the driver is?" Stern asked.

"I don't know," I said, "but you can be certain he's trying to get to Patriot Hills on foot."

"Bet he's got the idols, whoever he is. My money's on Zapata."

"I doubt we'll ever know. Alone out here he hasn't a chance. Both he and the statues are lost, I'd say."

"Scott." It was Esmeralda. I went over. She turned off her radio and gestured vaguely for me to do the same. She touched her helmet to mine. "I don't have much longer. Whatever that bug is, it's got me. I can hardly stand up. You have to get the rest out of here."

"I don't know the way."

"We're in a wide valley. Follow it until the hills on both sides disappear. Turn slightly right after that, but not too much. After an hour or so, if the weather permits, you should make out the lights of Patriot Hills. Just follow them in."

"How much longer?" I asked.

She didn't answer for some time. "I can't be sure," she said at last. "My best guess is seven hours, but it could be another eight or nine. Whatever you do, don't stop. Don't stop for anything."

"All right. Is there anything else I can do?"

"Get them out of here alive, Scott."

A few minutes later she announced we were setting out. Ainsworth complained he couldn't go on, and Kira refused to move. Both Stern and I urged them to move, and finally—slowly—they did.

Our pace was much reduced now, a combination of general fatigue—it was midnight and we'd been at this since just after 10 that morning—plus the combination of the increasingly violent storm and, of course, illness. Esmeralda brandished her light from right to left every few minutes, searching for the bordering hills, but the snowfall restricted her vision. .

About an hour out, Ainsworth collapsed, toppling over as if he'd passed out. Kira immediately dropped to the snow in a sitting position as Pagan had done earlier.

"Esmeralda!" I called out. "Ainsworth's down."

While Stern spoke to an unresponsive Kira, I carefully knelt beside Ainsworth. I turned on my light and gasped at what I saw. The man's face was hideous, covered with pustules. Ominous black patches had now appeared, and he was salivating. His nose was running continuously. He mumbled something, but I didn't move closer to hear him, relying instead on my headset.

Stern came over. "How's Kira?" I asked.

He was staring at Ainsworth. "She looks the same. Scott, what is this? I've never seen anything like it." He sounded frightened.

"I don't know, I just don't know." A few feet away, I saw Esmeralda stretched out in the snow.

"Why don't *we* have it?" he asked. "Do you think we're going to get it?"

"I don't know the answer to that, either. I've got no symptoms. I'm just tired. You?"

"Exhausted, thirsty, hungry, but otherwise okay. What are we going to do?"

"The only thing we can do. Keep moving. We've got a long way to go yet. Check on Esmeralda, will you?"

I turned my attention back to Ainsworth. "We'll be leaving soon. Can you manage to go?"

He shook his head. He spoke, but the only word I could make out was "finished."

"Why'd you kill her?" I asked. Again he muttered but I could make no sense of it. "Why'd you kill her?" I repeated.

This time I heard the word "didn't."

"You don't want to die with a lie on your lips, Ainsworth. Why'd you kill her?"

"Angel," he said. "Angel did it."

"But you ordered it." By now he was beyond repentance, regret, beyond truth even, if he'd ever been there. In his final minutes, he returned to the theme that had dictated the course of his life.

"I don't deserve this," he managed. "I...I..." He continued in this vein for a time, then, in a moment of lucidity energy seized him. "You, you and Quentin, carry me to Patriot Hills. I'll...I'll make you ri..."

I never heard the last and he never spoke again. He breathed through his mouth for a few more seconds, then, finally, that simply stopped—and he was dead.

Stern was with Esmeralda. "Ainsworth's dead," I told him. "How is she?"

"Not good."

"Esmeralda, what do you want to do?" I asked kneeling beside her.

"Ainsworth's dead, you say?"

"Yes, just now."

"Help me to my feet. I'll go a little more. I don't want to die beside that *hijo de puta*." Stern took her arm and lifted her. My light caught her face for an instant. It was hideous. I went to Kira.

"We're moving out. Are you coming?"

"Need to rest first." Her voice was faint.

"There's no resting here. Only dying. Come with us. Ainsworth's dead, Kira. You don't want to stay here." I reached down and with some effort managed to lift her to her feet. I glanced forward and saw Esmeralda step off. "Let's go." I gave Kira a gentle nudge, and she set out behind Stern.

I glanced at the temperature. Minus 101 degrees.

The storm was reaching a raging pitch. Visibility was reduced to a few yards and the effort of moving against the wind was exhausting. Powerful gusts, like invisible hands, pushed me to the side more than once.

We'd been moving for perhaps five minutes when Esmeralda stopped, swayed on her feet then collapsed. I went up to her, but there was nothing to say. She needed a miracle—and we were fresh out. I knelt beside her but didn't lift her visor. I didn't want to see her lovely face in this condition.

"Can I do anything for you?" I asked.

"Just leave me. I can't go on."

"Is there anything I can do?"

"Tell my parents about Ignacio and me. Tell them…Tell them I'm sorry. I never should have come here in winter. It's too much. I just…I just wish…"

"What?"

"I just wish I knew that Carlos was dead."

After that she prayed. I went over to Stern, who was with Kira. "She's unconscious," he said.

I went back to Esmeralda but found her dead. I took her hand-held light and returned to Stern. "We should leave, Quentin. There's no hope here."

He turned to his ex-wife. "Kira, honey. Let's go. You have to stand up."

At first there was no reply, then I heard, "Go to hell. Leave me alone. I feel terrible."

"Come on. You have to stand up."

"Get the idols, okay? I'll split it with you."

"Kira," I said. Time to clear up a few things. "What happened to Carlos?" She made a sound like a laugh.

"He's gone, no problem. Wanted it all. So easy..."

"Honey," Stern said again. "Let me help you up."

"Go away," she said irritably.

"Think of Samantha. Please. Stand up."

"Quentin, you're so lame. Leave me alone."

"Come on," I said. "We have to leave. We've a long hike yet."

Stern straightened up. "Goodbye, Kira. I really did love you."

"Quentin," she managed. "Go to hell."

We passed Esmeralda with Stern hiking beside me. We'd gone perhaps a mile when he finally spoke. I was prepared for something about Kira, about his marriage. Instead he asked, "How long is it?"

"Six to ten hours, I think."

"So far? I don't know if I can make it."

"We've no choice."

After a few steps he asked again, "Why aren't we sick?"

"Give it time."

"I think...I think if I get sick I'll just take my helmet off and let the cold do its business. I don't want to die like that." He had a point. A few minutes later he said, "Do you think you can find Patriot Hills in this soup?"

I flashed the light to our right and saw nothing but snow, then to our left with no results. "I have no idea."

Fifteen

Mercifully, an hour later, the snow began to ease, though the wind did not. The beam of my light managed to touch a hill to our left, enough to satisfy me we were generally headed in the right direction. My suit still functioned, though I had the sense that it was less responsive to my changing exertions and the wind conditions. There were times when I was very cold, others when I was too hot and opened my visor to vent heat. Stern and I didn't discuss it, but I saw him raising and lowering his visor, as well. At least the suit hadn't ceased functioning, as it had twice before.

We'd been on our feet for 19 hours with no significant break. But we were close to our destination, and I was beginning to let myself think we could manage it, assuming the suits held out and we didn't bypass Patriot Hills. The temperature stood at minus 99 degrees.

Try as I might to empty my thoughts I found it impossible. Too much had happened. I didn't want to think about what had killed Ainsworth, Esmeralda and Kira, but their images floated relentlessly my mind.

What if Stern had been right? This was unlike any disease I'd ever seen. Had the Chilean scientists raised something deadly from the icy core of Antarctica, some primeval plague for which we humans had no immunity? It was either that or some type of biological weapon. I couldn't think of another explanation.

I was inclined to believe that the scientists had inadvertently contaminated us, but there was no reason to dismiss the possibility that one of Ainsworth's many enemies had found a way to introduce a deadly bug into the expedition. If so, then it really was just a matter of time before Stern and I came down with it. The skeleton crew at Patriot Hills was likely sick or dead already. Without maintenance, I wondered if the shelters there would even be habitable, and if communications would work.

I kept to Esmeralda's pace and stopped every hour for five minutes. Neither of us had much to say when I did. This was the third time we'd come down from a summit among the few survivors, this time as the *only* ones. The first had been on Mt. McKinley, the other Aconcagua. We were making a habit of it.

"We aren't climbing any more mountains together," I said.

"The way I feel, I doubt that's going to be a problem. And have you considered that Patriot Hills may be as dead as Camp Two was? Maybe the two guys left there to run it are already dead. I don't know how much of the system was automated or how long it would run on its own. Do you have any idea when the plane is due back? Do we have to call out for it?"

It told him that I had no idea.

Six hours after we'd left Esmeralda and Kira I could see nothing ahead of us. This was the earliest time when it might be possible to reach Patriot Hills. We'd cleared the low-lying hills to our flanks. I'd turned to our right and from then on kept a close watch for the telltale glow in the night that would serve as a beacon for our salvation—but there was nothing. Nothing.

The wind changed direction, telling me the spiraling storm was moving by us. Though diminished the falling snow continued limiting my vision, but from time to time there were patches when visibility was greatly increased, though I still didn't see the glimmering I was searching for.

Two grueling hours later, however, off to our left, I spotted a dim light bobbing in the darkness. I stopped and watched it in fascination before realizing what I was seeing. It was a helmet light and meant we'd overtaken whoever had murdered those at Camp

Two. Somehow whoever it was had managed to stay on roughly the same track we were following.

"Do you see it?" Stern asked.

"Yes."

"He's angling towards the way we're going."

"I think he's spotted us and decided we know something he doesn't."

"Who is it?"

"Zapata? We'll soon find out."

"Look!" Stern all but shouted. I turned my attention back to our route and there, in the distance, off to our right, was a faint glow. "That's got to be it!"

"Yes. That's it." I checked the time. 7:09 A.M. I altered course and made for it, keeping my eye on the faint moving light to our left. It was ahead, and I realized now that it was not striking a course to intercept us but had spotted Patriot Hills before we had.

"Can you pick up the pace?" I asked. "I think we should try and get there before he does."

"I'll try, but I'm really, really beat."

"We'll walk fast for 100 steps, then at our normal pace, then 100 fast, then normal again. Let's go."

Anyone watching us would have found the idea that we were moving significantly faster ludicrous. The old military system was to run 100 paces, then walk, then run, and so forth. We weren't up to that. And tired as we were, we were not moving at any great pace. But it was faster than we had been.

I found accurate distance perception was impossible with no reference points. I soon realized that we were much closer to the other climber than I'd thought. I wondered what the range of our radios was by this time, if there was any point in trying to talk to him.

Despite the fact that we were moving at only a modest pace, my legs were soon burning, and I welcomed the respite every 100 steps. Our suits were overheating, and each of us opened our visor, leaving it open for longer periods and more often. Stern was dropping behind me, and I didn't want to be separated from him,

but then I didn't want to get to Patriot Hills after the other man either, so I pressed on.

Our goal drew nearer, but I wondered if I had the strength to keep this up. Whoever was ahead of us had started from Camp Two, much closer than we, then had ridden a considerable distance before being forced to walk. He was fresher than either of us.

One hundred fast steps, one hundred normal. My legs screamed in agony and I was burning up in the suit.

I glanced behind me. Stern had dropped well back. "Go ahead," he said. "Don't wait for me." He bent at the waist like an exhausted marathoner.

As I drew nearer, the shelters at Patriot Hills shone in the night, though they lacked the translucence of the habitats. Bright lights streamed from the windows of two of them, while the others sat in near darkness. The man I was chasing reached the main shelter well ahead of me. I realized that in my weakened condition I'd never stood a chance.

Some minutes later, I arrived. I stopped, sucked air, then moved to one of the windows. Inside were the two men Bryan had left behind, one of them the burly radio operator I'd seen when I'd first arrived. And there, stepping out of the last of his suit was Zapata. I gasped at what I saw.

His face was a hideous mask. Pustules oozed from his forehead and cheeks, and his nose was streaming. Dark patches blotted his skin.

The pair inside had pulled away from him in horror. With the whistle of the wind, I couldn't make out what they were saying, but clearly the two men were not happy. Neither stepped forward to offer Zapata any assistance. He gestured toward the radio. The men looked at one another in concern, then slowly separated, presenting two targets a greater distance apart. Military, I thought. It was instinctive with them.

I spotted Stern arriving. Either he didn't see me or he didn't care what I was doing because he went straight for the entrance. "Wait!" I said but it was too late, he'd gone inside. I rushed to the front entrance and followed him in.

Zapata was startled by our sudden appearance, and I wondered if he'd seen us at all earlier. He moved toward the radio set with his back to it, keeping his body between the radio and the four of us. I kept my distance as I removed my helmet. Stern did the same.

"What's going on?" the burly one demanded.

"Zapata here killed everyone else," Stern answered.

"What?" the other said, staring wild-eyed at us.

Zapata, standing in his long johns, was breathing deeply, sucking air into his ragged lungs, leaning forward to cough and spit up every few seconds. There were dark spots on his clothing, as if his insides were oozing out. He was having trouble tracking as his eyes went in and out of focus. He belonged in quarantine in a hospital. He was weaving back and forth on his feet, as if he might pass out at any second.

"He found a way to infect the suits with the disease," I said. "Ainsworth, Kira and Esmeralda all died from it. Pagan's suit failed, so I guess we can't lay that at his feet."

"And he killed the rest at Camp Two," Stern said. "He cut the habitats open and let them freeze to death!"

The pair stared at Zapata with a look of horror and anger. "What about Bryan?" the first man asked.

"Zapata stabbed him," I said. The second man made a move toward Zapata. "Don't," I said. "He'll infect you."

Zapata leaned down, then reached into the bag. I heard a clinking sound, then caught the tantalizing glint of gold. From the bag he pulled a revolver, which he now pointed at us. It was dripping in moisture as it heated up, a faint steam radiating from it.

The burly one looked to the other then said, "It's frozen. I don't think it'll fire." But neither man moved. I certainly didn't. I'd read somewhere that despite the simplicity of operation, the interior workings of revolvers were vulnerable to extreme cold. Regardless, the weapon I feared wasn't a handgun; it was the disease crawling across Zapata's skin.

"Call in the airplane," Zapata croaked. "Do it! And tell them to bring a medical team."

"The plane's due tomorrow—unless the weather prohibits it or we tell it to delay. We're filing weather reports every hour. The way things stand, if conditions don't improve, there will be no airplane."

The other man spoke to me. "What you said before, are you certain? All those people are dead?"

"We're certain," I said.

He looked at his colleague. "I guess this explains why we haven't heard from the Chilean Research Station. They've been off the air for two days."

"I said call in the airplane! Declare a medical emergency." Zapata waved his gun around like a magic wand. "You've got a sick man who needs help."

"I'm telling you, they don't care," the first man said. "They aren't risking a landing in these conditions. The storm is moving through, but the earliest it will clear out is late tonight. As I told you, we expect the plane tomorrow—unless we're wrong about the storm."

"I don't have a day!" Zapata shouted. "I can't wait!" He swayed. "I said get on the radio now!"

The pair looked at one another again, then the first spoke. "Then move away from it."

"What? Afraid it's catchy?" But Zapata moved closer to the entrance.

"Was it worth it, Evo?" I asked.

"Stay where you are," he ordered, pointing the gun at me.

"I'm not coming anywhere near you," I said. "I just want to know if killing everyone was worth it. And how'd you do it?"

The radio operator had the earphones on and was making his call.

"You're so smart, Mr. CIA, you tell me."

"All right. Chavez has a connection to the Chilean military, and one of the scientists gave you a sample of whatever it was they discovered over there. When Bryan's team was inspecting the suits, you infected them. That's why you were so eager to watch what they were doing. And you weren't sick at the time. You faked it to stay behind."

"Not bad. But there was nothing I could do about Ainsworth. Pagan wouldn't let me near their suits. Where are they?"

"We told you. They're dead. Ainsworth died from what you have, and Pagan's suit failed."

"Really? I don't…I don't see…" He swayed then turned to the radio operator. "When are they coming?"

"I can't raise Arenas. It's been a problem since the storm arrived."

"Keep trying!" He turned back to us. "Bryan inspected their suits. Maybe he did it."

"Could he get any of the stuff? Maybe Ainsworth caught it from one of the others. Pagan didn't have it, from what I saw."

"What about all those people at Camp Two?" Stern shouted. "Why did they have to die?"

"What else could I do? I found the idols where Kira stashed them. It wasn't hard. She was just a stupid woman. Bryan and his men weren't going to let me take them, were they? I had no choice. This was all Ainsworth's doing. If he'd just done what he promised, none of this would have happened. None of it."

"How'd you do it?" Stern asked.

Zapata's laugh came out like a bark. He coughed violently then spit out a great gob of goo. He was sweating profusely. "It wasn't hard, not at those temperatures. I sliced each habitat open and killed the power source. I was surprised at how fast they froze, how quickly all motion ended. No one even so much as left one of them. Bryan was out already. I had to deal with him, but he had no weapon, so it wasn't difficult."

"What about Carlos?" Stern asked. Kira told me she'd killed him.

"I never saw him. I don't know what happened. He's still out there, if he isn't with you."

"Did you sabotage the ETVs?" I said.

He laughed, then wiped is face with his sleeve. "No. I guess the U.S. military isn't so smart after all, is it?" He turned to the radio operator. "Are you through to them?"

"I'm trying."

"Hurry up! They need to get here today!"

"I'm telling you that with this storm they can't possibly arrive today, and even tomorrow may be out of the question."

"Just do it!"

"Evo, come on. It's over," I said. "Let's get you in bed where you belong. You need rest. We've got antibiotics here somewhere. Let's get you treated. The plane's already scheduled. This is the end of the world. You can't snap your fingers and expect things to happen."

"What are you doing?" Zapata shouted at the other man, who was moving deeper into the shelter, putting some distance between himself and the hideous creature brandishing a gun.

"Nothing. I'm just standing right here."

That was when the radio operator reached over and struck Zapata's forearm hard. Zapata pulled away, unfortunately keeping the revolver, which he leveled at the burly man and fired. The bullet went through his head with a splash of bone and brain, then continued into the radio that rested on the shelf behind him.

"No!" the other man shouted. "No!"

Though he was doing nothing but shouting, Zapata pointed the gun at him. I poked Stern and the two us bolted for the doorway as we heard the next gunshot.

Sixteen

We ran several yards into the storm and night then turned to watch the entrance to the shelter as we hurriedly put on our helmets and snapped the faceplates into place. My ears, cheeks and nose were already numb. Just then Zapata staggered outside, spotted us, and fired.

"This way," I said tugging at Stern's arm as I moved away from Zapata. The man had clearly lost his mind. He was staggering about like a drunk. No suit, just the gun in his hand, which he pointed at us and fired off another couple of rounds.

"Keep moving" I ordered. "He hasn't got long."

We drew away into the darkness, where there was no light of any kind. Zapata ran toward where we'd been but couldn't spot us in the vast expanse of Antarctica. He fired again, blindly.

"What's he doing?" Stern asked.

"He doesn't want to go alone. I've seen it before. You know you're dying and you want to take along company. This way." I moved us even farther away.

Zapata was now a ghostly black figure against the light of the shelter, partially obscured by the falling snow. Without a suit, at this temperature, in his sickened condition, the end couldn't take long. As we watched, he stopped moving altogether, standing perfectly still, like a stone sentinel. Finally, he toppled to the snow where he lay motionless. I waited several minutes as the wind and snow continued. Finally, I approached him cautiously. He lay inert, unmoving. When I reached him I kicked the weapon away, but it hardly mattered.

Zapata might still have been alive. I don't know. I wasn't going to get close enough to make certain. I also wasn't going to drag him into the shelter. From where I stood he didn't seem to be breathing. The snow was now clinging to his skin, suggesting it was no longer warm.

Stern arrived and went around to the other side. He knelt down so he could stare into the victim's face. "He looks dead."

"Probably. As good as."

"Now what?"

"Let's see about the other guy. Maybe Zapata missed."

He hadn't. The second man had been shot in the chest and died almost at once. I moved the burly man from the radio and confirmed that it was inoperable. When I looked up, Stern had removed the three golden idols from Zapata's bag, the cause of all this death and mayhem. He sat them in line on the table beside two cups of cold coffee.

"They're really something. Wish I had a camera. I wonder how many deaths they've witnessed over the centuries?"

Everyone seemed to ask that question. "More than we'll ever see, I hope."

Stern sat before them, quietly, and stared into the emerald green eyes. He didn't share his thoughts, but I was certain Kira, both good and bad, was in them somewhere. After a few minutes I went back outside. Zapata was nearly covered with the new snow that was falling more heavily now. There was no question that he was dead. Moving back inside, I said, "Let's get these others in the deepfreeze."

Stern nodded and helped me with the bodies, which we laid outside, beside the shelter, away from Zapata. I didn't want to run any risk of contamination, even in death, so these two could be buried beside their families instead of being incinerated.

Once we were back inside Stern asked, "What now?"

"Let's get some food, then sleep. We'll figure it all out later."

"How are we going to call out for a plane?"

"We don't have to. One's scheduled."

"But they won't hear from us."

"All the more reason for them to come. Let's get out of here."

The other shelter was for dining, though there were two beds set up for the use of the two murdered men. Given the state of the other shelter, we decided to wait here for the plane. I found water, which we both drank until we were nearly sick. I heated four cans of stew, and we wolfed the food down standing up.

After that, Stern crawled into one of the beds and was asleep instantly. Much as I wanted to do the same, I forced myself to re-dress, then went back out in the now raging storm and made my way to Ainsworth's quarters. I searched for ten minutes but found nothing. I'd hoped for a sat phone. I returned to the shelter, undressed, and finally went to bed.

I slept nearly 24 hours, and when I did wake up, Stern was still out of it. The storm had stalled and was still raging outside without letup. There'd be no plane for the time being. I set about fixing a large breakfast, and the smell of food got him up. As we ate, he said, "How did Evo get infected?"

"My guess is he did it to himself by accident. It wouldn't be the first time."

"Do you think we're going to get sick?"

"I doubt it, at this point. We'd be dead already if we had it."

He ate a bite or two of food, then asked, "When do you think the plane will come?"

"After the storm."

Thirty-six hours later, after the storm had finally passed and the sky above was a brilliant canopy of stars, we heard the roar of jet engines as a USAF C-17 Globemaster made a low, slow pass overhead. The temperature was standing at minus 56 degrees, almost summer-like for Patriot Hills.

We went to the control room where Stern switched on the runway lights. Though covered by the recent snow I could make out their glow. So could the plane, which made a lazy circle and then came in for a landing.

It was no surprise when U.S. military personnel stepped off the plane. They were ready for what they encountered as it was a special germ warfare unit. They wore no patches, so I couldn't identify the unit. Stern and I were placed in quarantine, then later transported to a military hospital in the States. Neither of us came down sick. I was debriefed endlessly as, I assume, was Stern. I learned later that the ETVs and other equipment abandoned near Vinson Massif were recovered. I was told that the Chilean military had given up its experiment with biological warfare. I assumed our military had taken it over.

Stern never wrote about the expedition. I've often wondered what they said to him.

As for the idols, I turned those over to the highest ranking officer on the recovery team and told him to contact Martin.

That's how I ended up on Kilamanjaro with the U.S. president a few months later.[5]

---

5   See *Murder on Kilamanjaro.*

Historical Overview

The Seven Summits and Their History Makers

- Everest
- Elbrus
- Mt. McKinley
- Puncak Jaya
- Aconcagua
- Vinson Massif
- Kilimanjaro

Mount Everest

The title "World's Highest Mountain" belongs to Mount Everest, located in the Mahalangur section of Himalayas on the Nepalese-Chinese border. It rises a stunning 29,029 feet—nearly 5.5 miles above sea level. To reach the summit is a lofty accomplishment, tackled by few and finished by even fewer.

The Himalaya mountains are considered to be an Asian range, although they quite literally separate the Indian subcontinent from the Tibetan Plateau—east to west from the Indus River valley to the Brahmaputra River Valley—thus creating a formidable physical barrier between the Nepal/Tibet and the Republic of China borders. The entire range consists of a 1,491 mile long arc, 93 miles wide, and it is home to the "Eight-Thousander" mountains, imposing peaks that includes both Mount Everest and K2 (also known as Nanga Parbat), which is the second highest mountain in the world.

In 1865, Mount Everest was given its official English name by the British Royal Geographical Society. Andrew Waugh, the British Surveyor General of India at the time, named it after his predecessor, Sir George Everest. The local Tibetans still call it *Chomolungma*, which translates as 'Saint Mother' or 'Mother Goddess of the Universe'.

Prior to its christening as Mount Everest by Waugh, the imposing giant was simply called Peak XV. Waugh helped to define Mount Everest as the tallest peak in the 1850s, taking the title from *Kangchenjunga.* George Everest himself opposed naming the mountain in his honor. He contended that the word "Everest," could not be written or pronounced in Hindi. His official objection was presented to the Royal Geographical Society in 1857, but despite Everest's objections, Waugh's proposed name for the peak prevailed, and in 1865 the Royal Geographical Society officially adopted the name.

Naming confusion regarding Mount Everest continued into the 1960s, when the Nepalese government changed the official name in Nepal to *Sagarmatha,* which translates to "Goddess of the Sky", and declared both *Chomolungma* and Everest as henceforth unrecognized names. Prior to the 1960s, this name had never been used and it never did really catch on; currently, the locals (both Nepalese and Tibetan) still stubbornly continue to recognize the peak as *Chomolungma.*

Mount Everest offers two main climbing routes: the southeast ridge from Nepal, and the northeast ridge from Tibet. The southeast ridge is technically easier and is used more frequently. This was the route used by New Zealand's Edmund Hillary and Nepalese guide Tenzing Norgay on the famous first summit conquest of Everest on May 29, 1953.

There is a small window of time during which climbers are able to summit Everest. Most attempts are made in the month of May, before the summer monsoon season begins. During this period, average wind speeds are reduced, making the climb safer. Some climbers also attempt to summit after the monsoon season, during September and October. Unfortunately, there is likely to be extra snow on the approach to the summit, and the weather patterns are less stable during this secondary window of opportunity.

Mount Everest History Makers

In 1921, the first attempt to summit Mount Everest occurred. Englishman George Mallory discovered the North route on Everest. He led the expedition and became the first European to set foot on the flanks of the mountain. Mallory's expedition reached 22,989 feet above sea level before needing to turn back. On his second expedition to Everest, in 1922, Mallory again attempted to summit using the North route. Because he was leading the expedition, Mallory is faulted for the deaths of seven native porters who were killed in an avalanche. Mallory was also pulled down by the avalanche but was able to survive.

Mallory made his final expedition to Mount Everest in 1924. His initial attempt to summit via the North-East ridge route was aborted because of extreme weather conditions at camp VI. Then, on June 8, 1924, Mallory began his final attempt to summit the mountain but never returned. His body, which lay on the North Face in a snow basin below and to the west of Camp VI, was not found until May of 1999 by the Malloy and Irvine Research Expedition.

The first successful ascent of Mount Everest belongs to Sir Edmund Hillary of New Zealand. In 1953, Hillary (age 33) and Sherpa mountaineer Tenzing Norgay became the first climbers known to have reached the summit of Mount Everest. Hillary and Norgay were part of the ninth British expedition to Everest and summited from the Nepal side of the mountain. Their expedition included more than 400 people, including 362 porters, 20 Sherpa guides, and approximately 10,000 pounds in baggage.

The last stretch before climbers reach the summit of Mount Everest has been named Hillary Step after Sir Edmund. In accomplishing this task, Hillary and Norgay clung to the rock wall as they slowly ascended to the summit. The two reached the top of the world between 1:00 and 1:30 a.m., but they stayed for only about 15 minutes.

News of the ascent reached Britain on the day of the coronation of Queen Elizabeth II. The press called the summit a 'gift' to the royal family. Afterwards, 37 members of the expedition received a coronation medal, engraved with "Mount Everest Expedition" on its rim. Hillary was also knighted by the Queen, and Norgay received the British Empire Medal. Ever since his expedition was so honored, Hillary's image has also been featured on the New Zealand five-dollar note.

Following his ascent of Everest, Hillary devoted his life to helping the Sherpa people of Nepal through a trust he founded and called the Himalayan Trust. Through his efforts, many schools and hospitals were built in the more remote regions of the Himalaya Mountains.

On April 30, 1985, Dick Bass became the first person to reach the summit of every one of the Seven Summits. At that time he also held the record for being the oldest person to have climbed Mount Everest. After his successful summit of Everest and the other mountains in the Seven Summits group, Bass co-authored a novel called *Seven Summits,* which detailed his adventures.

There is controversy surrounding Bass' completion of the Seven Summits. Depending on the geographical, geologic or geopolitical definitions, the highest summit of Europe is either Mont Blanc (France, 4807 m.), or Elbrus (Russia, 5662 m.). The polemic is even stronger for the 7th summit in Oceania, with either Kosciuszko (Austrailia, 2228 m.) or the Carstensz Pyramid (Indonesia, 4884 m.). Today there are two "official" lists of the 7 Summits: Bass' version, with Kosciuszko as 7th summit, and the Messner's list, with the Carstensz Pyramid as 7th summit. In both cases, Elbrus is considered as the top of Europe. Currently, 1996 holds the record of being the deadliest year on Mount Everest. Fifteen climbers died that year, eight of them in the same incident, on May 11. Researchers believe that odd weather circumstances caused many of the May 11 deaths, and they also estimate that the oxygen levels dropped to 14 percent.

There are numerous and varied records held by climbers of Mount Everest. The youngest person to summit was 13-year-old Jordan Romero in May, 2010; Apa Sherpa holds the record for reaching the summit the most times—20 as of May, 2010. The fastest ascent, made in 2007, belongs to Christian Stangl, an Austrian climber, who completed the distance in 16 hours and 42 minutes. The oldest climber to summit was 76-year-old Min Bahadur Sherchan in May, 2008. In 1988, Jean-Marc Boivin of France descended Mount Everest in 11 minutes by paragliding down.

Mount Elbrus

Mount Elbrus, a dual-summit mountain, lies within the western Caucasus mountain range in Russia, near the politically strife-ridden border between Russian and Georgia. The range stretches from the Caspian Sea to the Black Seas and creates a natural boundary between the Russian steppes and the three southern states of Azerbaydzhan (Azerbaijan), Georgia, and Armenia.

Mount Elbrus stands as the highest mountain in Europe, with its western summit rising to 18,510 feet above sea level. The mountain also has an east summit that reaches 18,442 feet in elevation. Within the list of the Seven Summits, Mount Elbrus is the fifth highest.

In addition to being the fifth highest of the Seven Summits, Mount Elbrus is volcanic. It is considered to be inactive, but beneath the mountain there still resides a large supply of active magma. There has never been a documented eruption, but scientists believe the physical evidence indicates that the last eruption may have occurred sometime in the first century A.D. The mountain shows signs of solfataric (an opening in the earth's crust) activity, and as a result, the area has numerous hot springs.

According to myth, Mount Elbrus was known as 'Strobilus' to ancient civilizations, which believed that Zeus had chained Prometheus, the Titan, to the mountain, because he stole fire from the gods to give to the people. This is thought to be an indirect reference to some historic volcanic activity.

Mount Elbrus provides two main routes to its summit. The Normal, or traditional, route is the most frequently used. It is the easiest, safest and fastest way to the summit. This is because of a cable car and chairlift system that carries climbers most of the way up the mountain. A longer ascent to the summit is to be found along the Kiukurtliu Route. This starts from below the cable car terminal, and climbers travel over glacial slopes towards the Khotiutau pass. Still other climbers have attempted Elbrus from the northwest and Periwal Balkashi side. This is far more difficult and therefore is less used.

According to theory, the name Elbrus is derived from the Persian name 'Alborz'. The word Alborz, in turn, is taken from the name of a mountain in Persian mythology, Hara Barezaiti, which translates to 'High Watch' or 'High Guard'. Other names for the mountain include *Mingi Taw,* meaning 'Thousand Mountain' in Turkic, *Oshkhamakhua,* meaning 'The Mount of Happiness' in Circassian, and *Ialbuzi,* its equivalent in the Georgian dialect.

In more recent history, Mount Elbrus has been subject to interesting acts of war. The mountain was included in a war-zone during World War II. During 1942, the German Army, the *Wehrmacht,* occupied the area surrounding the mountain with 10,000 troops. A Soviet pilot bombed the German fuel supply on the mountain. In retaliation, the general in command of the troops on Mount Elbrus sent a climbing party to the summit and placed the Swastika flag there. Surprisingly, Adolf Hitler, enraged by the act, called it a stunt and threatened to court-martial the general if it was not taken down.

Mount Elbrus is one of the deadlier mountains among the Seven Summits. The average annual death toll on Elbrus is 20 to 30 lives. Elbrus authorities attribute the high loss total to many climbers not being properly prepared or equipped for the arduous climb. Many novice mountaineers see Mount Elbrus as an 'easy' climb because of the cable car. This leads to mistakes on the mountain, many of which result in fatal errors in judgment. For example, climbers attempting to summit the mountain too fast may incur high altitude cerebral edema (HACE). As climbers ascend to higher elevations, oxygen levels continue to drop. If climbers ascend too quickly and do not acclimate to the reduced levels of oxygen, the brain swells, which can result in seizure, paralysis, coma and death.

Sudden storms are also common. Thunderstorms and 'white-outs' can happen sporadically on Elbrus. Whiteouts occur when the snowfall intensifies such that visibility and contrast are severely reduced. In such cases, the horizon and all location reference points disappear completely, leaving climbers disoriented. Caught in whiteouts, some lose the path and are often never found again. Clearly, aspiring climbers should also be prepared for extreme cold weather on Elbrus. Frostbite and hypothermia have affected many people attempting to summit this tricky mountain.

Climbers are required to obtain three permits to scale Mount Elbrus. Foreign climbers will need a Border Zone Permit just to be in the area south of Badsan, and they will also need to be registered in OVIR in Tyrnauz. OVIR registration is required by travelers staying in Tajikistan for the period of three days and longer. The Department of Visas and Registration of the Ministry of Internal Affairs will give you OVIR registration stamps. And finally, a Prielbrusie National Park Permit is required for access to the park.

Elbrus History Makers

The lower of the two summits was first reached on July 10th, 1829, by Khillar Khachirov, a Karachay guide for the Imperial Russian Army climbing expedition. The Russian troop was part of a scientific expedition led by General Emmanuel.

The west and higher summit of Mount Elbrus was reached in 1874 by an English expedition led by Florence Crauford Grove. Grove was an experienced mountaineer and a member of the Alpine Club of London. After his ascent, Grove wrote *The Frosty Caucasus: An Account of a Walk Through Part of The Range and of an Ascent of Elbruz in the Summer of 1874* [sic]. *The Frosty Caucasus* gives detailed explanations of the mountain range and of the expedition.

Grove describes the climb to the summit of Mount Elbrus this way: "The valley grew narrower and more striking as we advanced, and there were wonderful glimpses up side gorges of snow-peaks so lofty and so great that it was difficult to understand how there was room for their foundations in the narrow glens whence they seemed to rise."

Russia has always encouraged ascents of Mount Elbrus. During the early years of the Soviet Union, mountaineering became a popular sport in the country. Then, in 1956, the USSR orchestrated an attempt by 400 mountaineers to summit Elbrus. This event was created to celebrate the 400th anniversary of the incorporation of Kabardino-Balkaria, a federal subject of Russia. In 1959, Russia began to build a cable car system to take visitors to various points on the mountain, the highest being 12,500 feet. The project was not finished until 1976. In 1997, a Land Rover Defender was driven to the summit, an accomplishment that has been recognized in the *Guinness Book of World Records.*

Mt. McKinley

Towering over the Denali National Park and Preserve in Alaska, Mount McKinley rises 20,320 feet above sea level, and is the tallest mountain in the United States (and North America). Mount McKinley is in the Alaska Mountain Range, which stretches from east to west across the southern portion of the state. Along the slopes of McKinley lie five large glacier flows: Peters Glacier, Muldrow Glacier, Traleika Glacier, Ruth Glacier, and Kahiltna Glacier.

Mount McKinley, like Mount Elbrus, has two significant summits. The South Summit is the higher, 20,320 feet, and is the peak included in the list of the Seven Summits. The North Summit rises 19,470 feet, and is much less climbed, than its sister summit. On average, 1,000 climbers attempt the South Summit each season; but only half reach the top and, on average, three perish on the mountain each year.

The weather on Mount McKinley can change rapidly and is notably unforgiving of mistakes. Because it is close to Aleutian Low, a semi-permanent low pressure center, the weather on McKinley is unlike that of any other mountain. Extreme cold is its trademark. Temperature routinely falls to -40 degrees Fahrenheit, with high winds also common along its incline.

Long periods of clear skies on the mountain are traditionally accompanied by high winds. During these windy periods, much of the mountain is swept clean of snow, leaving behind solid ice.

The slippery slopes are exceptionally dangerous for climbers, and the Denali Pass and the upper part of the West Rib are notorious locations for accidents. Winds in excess of 100 miles per hour are common year-round. Eye witness reports confirm that climbers have been picked up off the mountain by the wind and flung down the slopes. These violent wind storms occur without warning, and experienced climbers routinely take cover at first suggestion of increased wind speed. Many of the climbing accidents in 1992, one of the deadliest years for McKinley, were caused by high-velocity winds.

North America's crown jewel mountain is also known for low pressure cyclonic systems, which originate from the Gulf of Alaska, sweeping in from the southwest. The strongest have been described as snow hurricanes. Generally, climbers will have at least twelve hours warning before the storm reaches the mountain. But the weather service messages do not always get through. This atypical weather was responsible for a climbing accident on the Karstens Ridge route in 1967 that claimed the lives of seven climbers. It is thought that the expedition either did not get the weather message—or disregarded it.

In comparison to Mount Everest, Mount McKinley has a higher rise of 18,000 feet. The rise of Everest is 12,000 feet. Because Mount Everest reaches a higher elevation, at 29,029 feet above sea level, it is considered the tallest mountain. Due to the rise and extreme weather found on McKinley, the mountain is often used as a training ground for climbers desirous of conquering Everest.

Currently, the name of Mount McKinley is under dispute. The Koyukon Athabaskan people, the American Indian tribes which inhabit the area around the mountain, refer to the peak as Dinale or Denali. From the native language, Denali translates to 'The High One'. The first English name on record applied to Mount McKinley was *Densmore's Mountain* or *Densmore's Peak,* named for a gold prospector, Frank Densmore. In 1889, Densmore praised the mountain for its beauty and "majesty." In 1897, gold prospector William Dickey renamed it "Mount McKinley" as political support for the then presidential candidate, William McKinley of Ohio. An account of Dickey's experiences on the mountain was published in the *New York Sun,* which added support of the name "McKinley." The current name dispute is being argued between the state of Alaska and the United States federal government. According to the Alaska Board of Geographic Names, the name is Denali, but the United States Board of Geographic Names has it listed as McKinley.

McKinley History Makers

The historic first European sighting of Mt. McKinley took place on May 6, 1794. George Vancouver was surveying the Knik Arm of the Cook Inlet and saw a "distant, stupendous mountain." Vancouver referenced Denali in a British journal.

The first recorded attempt to climb the giant mountain was undertaken by James Wickersham in 1903. He chose an approach that used Peters Glacier and the North Face, which is now known as the Wickersham Wall. This difficult route was not successfully climbed until 1963; it is highly prone to avalanche. In order to finance his expedition, Wickersham wrote and published a single issue of a newspaper called *The Fairbanks Miner,* dated May, 1903. Unfortunately, Wickersham had to abandon his climb at approximately 8,000 feet above the base. Judge Wickersham also chronicled his expedition in his book, *Old Yukon: Tails, Trails, Trial.*

The summit of Mount McKinley has been subject to several climbing scandals since the early 1900s. In 1906, famed explorer Dr. Frederick Cook claimed the first completed ascent of the mountain. His announcement was regarded with suspicion from the beginning. Cook claimed to have reached the summit with one companion, Ed Barrill. He provided pictures of himself atop a mountain as 'proof' of his summit, but; these pictures were later shown to be a lower peak 19 miles from Mount McKinley. Subsequently, in 1909, his summit claim was publically challenged by Robert Peary. Barrill then signed an affidavit agreeing that the two had not reached the summit of Mount McKinley. It has been reported that Barrill was paid to do so by Peary supporters. Barrill also produced a map of the fake summit, and since then, Cook's claims have conclusively been proven false through photographs and actual descriptions of Mount McKinley's summit.

The 1910 expedition of four local Alaskans has come to be known as the Sourdough expedition. Despite having no climbing experience or training, Tom Lloyd, Peter Anderson, Billy Taylor and Charles McGonagall claimed to have spent three months on McKinley, which culminated on the North Summit of the mountain. During their time on the mountain, the Sourdoughs worked to set up camps along the route. The *New York Times* ran an article regarding the equipment used on the Sourdough Expedition, emphasizing that the climbers had used home-made crampons, (which they called "creepers"), snowshoes, and long poles fitted with a steel hook at one end and a spike on the other. The Sourdough Expedition did not use any rope and were never secured to the mountain, as are climbers today. At the summit, the Sourdough climbers reported driving a 14-foot spruce pole into the ice and snow of the North Summit. After the Sourdough summit, much of the climbing community doubted the accomplishment claimed by the Alaskans. Their inexperience, lack of training, and rudimentary climbing materials did not inspire belief in the summit.

It was not until 1913 that their claim was verified when the South Summit was reached by a party led by Hudson Stuck, from which the 1913 climbers saw the Sourdough flagpole on the North Summit, which proved the validity of Sourdough claims. The expedition that reached the South Summit included Stuck, Walter Harper, Harry Karstens and Robert Tatum. The Stuck expedition approached and conquered McKinley using the Muldrow Glacier route.

According to Robert Tatum, "The view from the top of Mount McKinley is like looking out the windows of Heaven!"

While on the summit the Stuck expedition took measurements to measure accurately the elevation of the mountain. Using various types of barometers and thermometers, the climbers were able to proclaim that McKinley was 20,384 feet above sea level. They were very close. Today's sophisticated, satellite-based tools show a small difference of only 20,320 being the accurate altitude. While atop the summit, the 1910 expedition members used a tent support as a flagpole and raised a small American flag to fly in the McKinley wind. The flag was constructed while on the climb, hand-made from two silk handkerchiefs and the cover of a sewing bag.

Puncak Jaya

Puncak Jaya dominates the landscape of the island nation of New Guinea. It is the hightest of the peaks in the Sudirman Range. Although it is the highest mountain in Indonesia, as well as the highest island mountain in the world, it is the smallest of the Seven Summits. A mere four degrees in latitude from the world's equator, it stands at 16,024 feet of elevation from base to summit. Despite the fact that it is very close to the equator, snow and ice still adorn the sides of Puncak Jaya.

In fact, while the peak is free of ice, there are glaciers spread across its slopes. Carstensz Glacier and the Northwall Firn are the two largest and best-known. Being equatorial, the air temperature on the mountain rarely varies. On average, the temperature hovers between 32 and 33 degrees Fahrenheit. The weather at the base of Puncak Jaya, however, is a different story. New Guinea is a tropical island, covered mostly by lush rainforests. The highlands below the mountain experience daytime temperatures ranging between 75 and 85 degrees Fahrenheit and dropping to 45 degrees at night. The mornings are generally filled with sunshine, but climbers have near-daily experiences with afternoon rain showers. Farther up, because of the colder average temperatures, the rain turns into snow. Because the weather does not change seasonally, Puncak Jaya can be climbed at any time of the year.

Originally called Carstensz Pyramid, Puncak Jaya was first sighted and recorded on a map by Dutch explorer Jan Carstensz in 1623. On a rare clear day, Carstensz spotted snow on the peak of the mountain. The sighting went unverified for another two centuries, during which time Carstensz was ridiculed throughout Europe for believing there to be snow so near the equator.

The name Carstensz Pyramid is still used among many mountain climbers, but in the 1960s, when Indonesia took back control of the province from the Netherlands, the name was officially changed to an Indonesian appellation that means "Victory Mountain" (commemorating the emancipation of New Guinea from the Dutch colonial empire in 1963). The Dutch had controlled New Guinea since the mid-1800s as part of the Netherland Spice Island Empire. The Netherlands had intended to release control over New Guinea in the 1970s, but during the late 1950s the people of Indonesia began to exert additional pressure on the Dutch to expedite their emancipation. As a result, and with the help of the United Nations, Indonesia was able to accomplish this sooner.

At the time of emancipation, New Guinea first renamed the mountain to Puncak Soekarno or Puncak Sukarno, after the nation's first president. Later, the name was changed yet again to Puncak Jaya.

Puncak Jaya is known to be one of the more demanding of the Seven Summits climbs. It has the highest technical rating, and climbers should possess rock climbing skills. In order to summit Puncak Jaya, climbers must conquer the 'wall'. The wall of Puncak Jaya begins at a bowed angle of 10 to 15 degrees, but closer to the top it becomes almost perfectly vertical. Many climbers compare 'the wall' to jagged glass.

Aside from challenges to skill, the mountain provides many other obstacles for aspiring climbers. Because it lies within a dense tropical forest, climbers are not able to reach the base of the mountain by road or by air. They must spend five to six days making the 100-kilometer trek through the rainforest to reach the base of the mountain.

The surrounding forest is also inhabited by indigenous and primitive (and sometimes intrusive) tribes. The Dani tribe populates the Baliem Valley, which is at the base of Puncak Jaya. Not having been visited by non-indigenous people until the late 1930s, the Dani tribe has held onto many of its tribal traditions. The men wear distinctive gourds over their genitals, and the women wear grass skirts. Pigs and women are the most valued possessions to the men of the Dani tribe, and agriculture is centralized around sweet potatoes. Danis are the most colorful of New Guineas tribes in terms of their dress and appearance, and they are particularly fond of "dressing up" for war. Tribesmen will adorn their heads with headdresses of feathers and their noses with boar's tusks. Dani women are known for lacking fingers because when a family member in a Dani tribe passes away, all women relatives are expected to remove a portion of a finger.

The rain forests of New Guinea surrounding Puncak Jaya is known for its animal inhabitants. Both tree pythons and death adders live in the area. New Guinea's largest bird, the flightless cassowary, is large enough to disembowel a human with its sharp claws. Sticky webs also give homes to bird-eating spiders.

Puncak Jaya History Makers

The snowfield of Puncak Jaya was first reached in 1909 by a Dutch explorer, Hendrik Albert Lorentz. His team consisted of six indigenous Dayak Kenyah porters from Apo Kayan in Borneo. Lorentz was a part of three expeditions to New Guinea; in the last, he reached the snowfield on Puncak Jaya. The Lorentz National Park and Lorentz River in New Guinea are named after him.

It wasn't until 53 years later that the peak was reached. Austrian mountaineer Heinrich Harrer summited Puncak Jaya in 1962. He summited with three other expedition members, Philip Temple, Russell Kippax and Bert Huizenga. Temple, from New Zealand, had recently led an expedition into the area and had pioneered the access route to Puncak Jaya.

Throughout his life, Heinrich Harrer traveled to many parts of the world, including much of Western Europe, India, Tibet, New

Guinea, Alaska, and Africa. After his travels through New Guinea, Harrer penned *I Come From the Stone Age.* This memoir elaborated on the time he spent in New Guinea and summiting Puncak Jaya. Harrer wrote: "On Aigera I wanted to test my skills, in Himalayas I got to know loneliness, in Tibet unusual people. On the New Guinea Island I found everything altogether." In his lifetime, Harrer wrote over 20 books detailing his travels. *I Come From the Stone Age* and *Seven Years in Tibet* are his two most famous. *Seven Years in Tibet* is devoted to his time in Tibet and his experiences tutoring the 14th Dalai Lama. It was made into a movie starring Brad Pitt. Heinrich Harrer passed away on January 7, 2006, at the age of 93, in Austria.

Other noted climbers of Puncak Jaya include Ripto Mulyono and Frenky Kowass. Mulyono is a member of the Indonesian national climbing team. In 2005, he reached that peak for a record-setting 20th time. Mulyono also gave climbing lessons to Kowass, who was the climber who installed the first fixed rope system on the Normal Route up Puncak Jaya.

Aconcagua

Mount Aconcagua lies in the Southern Andes Mountains, in the Mendoza province of west-central Argentina. It is acclaimed as the highest point in the Western Hemisphere. The peak is located mostly in Argentina, but its western flanks back into the coastal lowlands of Chile. The name Aconcagua originated from the Quechua "Ackon Cahuak," which translate to "Sentinel of Stone."

Aconcagua is widely accepted as the highest Western Hemisphere peak; however, its precise elevation has been debated since the 20th century. According to the Military Geographical Institute of Argentina, the highest summit is 22,831 feet above sea level. Yet in January of 2001, Italian geologist Giorgio Poretti led a team of scientists to measure Aconcagua's height using an advanced Global Positioning System, (GPS), and the team reported an elevation of 22,840. Currently, this new figure is not recognized by the government of Argentina or by the National Geographic Society. Aconcagua's southern and lower summit has been reported to be at 22,736 feet. Both summits are connected by a ridge, Cresta del Guanaco, about a half mile long.

The Andes Mountains tower above the Southern Hemisphere as a result of the Nazca plate, a geologic formation that is shifting from beneath the Pacific Ocean and diving underneath South America. This collision creates consistent earthquakes, volcanic eruptions, and the uplift that became the incredible mountain:

Aconcagua. Although formed from a volcanic origin, the mountain itself is not active.

Extending to more than 4.25 miles above sea level, Aconcagua generates its own weather. A wide range of temperatures and weather conditions present themselves between late November and late February, from warm days to freezing nights, with snow, wind, and extremely low humidity. Clear days do not happen often, but on those cloudless, sunny days, climbers may see the Pacific Ocean from the summit. This proximity to the ocean is a large factor in creating the more violent weather that can affect climbers on Aconcagua. The frequent cloud cover at the summits has earned it the respectful nickname "*Viento Blanco.*" Wind storms on Aconcagua are common and fierce. Dozens of climbers have perished as a consequence of the unpredictable weather.

Although weather on Aconcagua can present obstacles for climbers, the mountain does not confront climbers with many technical challenges. Two bits of evidence: 1) a summit was almost completed by climbers on motorcycles taking the Normal Route; and 2) dogs have accompanied their owners to the summit.

The official climbing season for Aconcagua extends from November 15 to about March 15. Climbers will experience the best conditions between late November and late February. The two factors that dictate this calendar are weather and logistics. The weather during this preferred period is warmer in the Austral (Southern) Hemisphere, and the climate on Aconcagua is more stable. Also, climbers have access to necessary elements during this time, including mules, base camp supplies, porters, and other climbing essentials.

Aconcagua was officially conquered first in 1897 by a Swiss mountaineer, Matthias Zurbritten. Previous attempts had begun during the 1880s. Although the first summit is credited to Zurbritten, traces of the Inca civilization and culture have been found near the summit.

The passes surrounding Aconcagua historically gained traffic through military use. In the effort to liberate Chile from Spain, General Jose de San Martin had traveled the area frequently.

By 1950, most sides of Aconcagua had been climbed, and variants of the original routes have since been added, with a consistent increase in successful summits.

The Normal Route of Aconcagua is through a series of camps. Beginning at Base Camp, climbers advance up the glacier to Camp 1, then onward to Camp 2, which is perched on a plateau 15,500 feet above sea level. It is often at Camp 2 that climbers begin to feel the effects of the hazardous winds on the mountain. The views from this point are inspirational and include parts of the Andean chain of mountains. The final camp, Camp 3, is at 19,900 feet above sea level and is the final place to rest before the push to the summit. To reach the top from Camp 3, climbers must use the Guanacos Traverse, which consists of steep rock bands covered in icy snow. The best views at this point in the climb are found at dawn, when the sun is rising above the Andes Mountains. Finally, climbers continue up the traverse until they are standing upon the summit, 22,831 feet above sea level.

Aconcagua History Makers

Paul Gussfeldt attempted to summit Mount Aconcagua in 1883, but unfortunately, he failed. Gussfeldt was a German scientist and an experienced explorer of Africa and Arabia. His climb lead him up the northern portion of the mountain in the hope that because that side saw more sunlight, it would be free of snow and ice. Aconcagua was mostly a mystery during this time, meaning that much of the route in those early years of exploration was mapped through guesswork.

Gussfeldt's climbing equipment, as was the case with many early climbers, was rudimentary. The list of his personal equipment included: silk and woolen shirts, two pairs of underpants, two pairs of woolen socks, one pair of pants, leg warmers, knitted jacket, vest, two pairs of woolen cuffs, woolen gloves and a bandana. Modern mountaineering gear is much more advanced and specifically made for the subzero temperatures found on mountains such as Aconcagua.

The first recorded summit is attributed to the Fitzgerald expedition in January of 1897, more specifically to Matthias Zurbriggen, the Swiss expedition guide. This expedition was the first to use the Horcones valley approach. In mid-January, Zurbriggen had reached the ridge between the two summits and two days later, on the 14th, was able to summit alone. The entire expedition did not make it to the summit due to altitude sickness, so Zurbriggen accomplished the climb alone. In fact, he holds a number of records for first ascents, as well as the second ascent of Mount Cook. The route created by Zurbriggen is now called the Normal Route and is the most frequently used route on Aconcagua.

Currently, the record for the youngest climber to reach the summit of Aconcagua is held by Matthew Moniz of Colorado. Moniz completed Aconcagua at the age of 11, in December of 2008. In 2010, he was named the National Geographic Adventurer of the Year.

Vinson Massif

Vinson Massif deserves recognition as the highest mountain on the coldest continent on earth. Located in Antarctica and situated in the Sentinel Range of the Ellsworth Mountains, its peaks rise above the Ronne Ice Shelf not far from the base of the Antarctic Peninsula. The massif is about 750 miles from the South Pole, and its highest point is Mount Vinson.

The website of the acclaimed PBS television series, NOVA, describes the mountain this way: "Vinson dominates a landscape of stark purity, where nothing other than ice, snow, and barren rock stretch as far as the eye can see. Antarctica, with Vinson at its ceiling, is the coldest and driest desert on Earth, receiving less than two inches of precipitation per year. Most of the snow on the mountain arrived there on the wind, blown from other parts of the continent."

Weather on Vinson is controlled by the polar ice cap's high-pressure system. Climate conditions generally are stable, but high winds and snowfall can occur, as is true of any arctic climate. Sunlight prevails 24 hours a day during the summer season, which runs from November through January. The average balmy temperature during these months is minus 20 degrees Fahrenheit, but the harsh sun will melt snow on dark objects. Glaciers have formed over the eons as the snow has been compacted into ice.

Vinson Massif was first seen by human eyes in 1958, when it was spotted by passengers on a U.S. Navy aircraft flying out of Byrd Station. It was named for Carl Vinson, a Georgia U.S. congressman who had been a force in obtaining public funding for Antarctic research. The first climb of the massif did not take place for eight years, in 1966. An expedition in 2001 first climbed via the Eastern route. By February of 2010, 700 climbers had tried to reach the top of Mount Vinson, but only about 600 had succeeded.

The chief barrier to climbing the mountain is not technical, it is economic. Costs of a climb are exorbitant by any standard, especially the logistical expense of simply making it to the base of the mountain. Most guided trips cost about $30,000. Expeditions depart from Punta Arenas, Chile, the most prominent city on the Strait of Magellan, flying across Antarctica on a six-hour flight directly to Union Glacier, the base for Mount Vinson climbs. Formerly Patriot Hills was the base. From there, a one-hour flight takes climbers to the Vinson Massif base camp at 9,100 feet. Another thousand feet higher, Camp Two awaits. Camp Three, at 15,311 feet, is reached by climbing moderate snow slopes to the col between Vinson Massif and its nearest neighbor, Shinn. After a day or two of acclimatization, the summit is attempted with a three-mile traverse over snow slopes to the summit ridge, at which point, the summit is still 3,000 feet above the climbing party.

Vinson was first summited in 1966 by an American Alpine Club expedition. The event was well-publicized because, for a while, it was being touted as a "race" to the top. The AAC team was one of the two purported contestants. The other was supposed to be a group led by mountaineer Woodrow Wilson Sayre. The Sayre group, it was said, was planning to fly into the Sentinel Range in a Piper Apache piloted by Max Conrad, the "Flying Grandfather." Sayre had a questionable reputation because he had gone into Tibet without authorization from China in an unsuccessful and nearly fatal attempt to climb Mt. Everest from the north in 1962. As it turned out, the "race" did not come off because Conrad had problems with his plane. He and Sayre were still in Buenos Aires on the day the first members of the AAC group reached Vinson's summit on Dec. 18, 1966.

Vinson Massif History Makers

The first ascent of Vinson Massif was accomplished by two groups within the American Alpine Club that joined forces in 1966. In the forefront of the expedition were Charles Hollister, Samuel C. Silverstein, M.D., and Peter Schoening. Nicholas Clinch of Pasadena, Calif., was recruited to lead the climb.

Among the climbers, the most revered was Schoening, a mountaineering legend for his heroism in "The Belay," a feat of skill he carried out in August, 1953. At the time, Schoening was a member of a group attempting to climb K2 in the Himalayas, the world's second-tallest mountain; and considered by some to be a more difficult challenge than Mt. Everest. On the seventh day, climbing without oxygen, the group became trapped at over 25,000 feet on the Abruzzi Ridge. One member of the group developed severe blood clots in his left calf—a condition that could easily kill him if a clot broke loose.

In a raging storm, the climbers began to descend on Aug. 10, hauling their fallen comrade in a sleeping bag and on a shredded tent. Schoening was at the top of a steep slope, his ax planted behind a boulder and a rope passing over the boulder and ax and around Schoening's waist and hip. Suddenly, one of the climbers lost his footing, dragging another climber with him, then another, until six climbers were falling and tumbling down the mountain, on their way to certain death thousands of feet below. All that stood between them and death was Schoening, and he held. With his rope stretched pencil-thin, he stopped their fall. All survived, though the man with the blood clots was later swept away by an avalanche and disappeared.

Other celebrated climbers on the first Vinson Massif were Hollister and Clinch.

Hollister, a world-renowned marine geologist, was also a hunter, fisherman and alpine/cross-country skier. A native of Santa Barbara, California, he grew up on a family ranch that was once was one of the largest cattle ranches in the state. With an interest in climbing that began early in life, he climbed Mount Rainer in Washington while serving in the U.S. Army. In college, he tackled the Cascades and the Sierras, then continued on to other peaks in North America and around the world. In 1962, he took part in the first ascent of the southeast side of Mount McKinley in a month-long expedition. He not only climbed Vinson Massif but also ascended four other peaks in Antarctica's Sentinel Range, earning the John Oliver La Gorce Medal from the National Geographic Society for "contributions to science and exploration through the first ascent of Antarctica's highest mountains."

Clinch, a resident of Palo Alto, California, was regarded as one of America's most skilled expedition leaders. He had led the first ascent of Gasherbrum I, also known as Hidden Peak/K5 (located on the Pakistan-China border) (26,250 feet) in 1958, and Masherbrum (25,660 feet) in 1960, the two highest peaks first climbed by Americans. Hidden Peak is the only 8,000-meter peak first climbed by Americans. Clinch's account of the expedition was published as the book, *A Walk in the Sky*. His explorations included many ascents in the United States, the British Columbia Coast Range, Peru and China. He was made a Fellow of the prestigious Explorers Club in 1969, and received the American Alpine Club Gold Medal in 2006.

In addition to the more well-known Schoening, Hollister, Clinch and Silverstein, the other members of the expedition that first climbed Vinton Massif were J. Barry Corbet, John P. Evans, Eiichi Fukushima, William E. Long, Brian S. Marts and Richard Wahlstrom.

Kilimanjaro

With its three volcanic cones towering above the African plains, Mount Kilimanjaro stands 19,340 feet above sea level, and is the fourth highest peak in the Seven Summits. Kilimanjaro rests in the northeastern region of Tanzania, just south of the Kenyan border, and is the highest mountain in Africa. It is also considered the world's tallest free-standing mountain, and, when measured from base to summit, it is the fourth most prominent.

The three volcanic cones are: Kibo, the tallest, at 19,340 feet; Mawenzi, at 16,896 feet; and Shira, at 13,000 feet. In order to summit Kilimanjaro, climbers must tackle Kibo and reach Uhuru Peak, the highest summit on Kibo's crater rim.

Two of the three peaks on the mountain, Mawenzi and Shira are both volcanically extinct; Kibo, on the other hand, is considered to be dormant but could possibly erupt again. The most recent volcanic activity from Kilimanjaro was recorded approximately 200 years ago, and although it is currently considered inactive, Kilimanjaro has fumaroles that emit volcanic gas in the crater of the main summit. In 2003, scientists concluded that molten magma was present approximately 1,300 feet beneath the surface of the Kibo crater.

Kilimanjaro, like many such lofty peaks, creates its own weather system, encouraged by the 'trade' and 'anti-trade' winds. These are strong gusts that gain speed and moisture over the oceans.

Eventually, they hit Kilimanjaro and create the rainy and dry seasons on the mountain. The trade winds bring the mountain two rainy seasons each year—the "long rains" from March through May and a less intense rainy season from November to February, and the dry 'anti-trade' winds that hit the mountain from May to October. Due to its equatorial location, Mount Kilimanjaro does not experience a wide range of temperatures over the course of a year. Temperatures on the mountain itself are mostly determined by time of day and altitude. At the base of the mountain, the average daily temperature is 70 to 80 degrees Fahrenheit. As climbers progress up the slope, the temperature continues to drop. Naturally, it is coldest at its peak, which at night can reach zero to -15 degrees Fahrenheit. Both Kibo and Mawenzi are capped, all year long, by glaciers.

The origin of the name 'Kilimanjaro' has not been fully verified. Many believe the theory that the name began with the Chagga, the Tanzanian tribe that resides in the shadow of the mountain. As one word, Kilimanjaro does not resemble anything in the Chagga language. Yet when broken into two parts, it is possible to find a Chagga translation within the name. The first portion, 'Kilima,' may be derived from the Chagga term 'kilelema,' meaning 'difficult or impossible,' while 'njaro' is similar to 'njaare,' which translates to 'bird.' In rough translation, Kilimanjaro could be inferred to mean '*That which is impossible for the bird*'—speaking to the enormity of the mountain. Modern-day Chagga people do not have an exact word for the mountain. Instead, they see Kilimanjaro as two separate mountains; specifically, Mawenzi and Kibo. In the Chagga language, Mawenzi translates to 'having a broken top' and Kibo to 'snow'.

The Chagga were not officially formed into one, cohesive people until World War II. In 1924, there were over 732 Chagga clans living at the base of Mount Kilimanjaro. Over time, family ties began to die and the clans dwindled. Eventually, after tribal wars and the continued familial die-off, the number of tribes had decreased to six. From the six tribes, a common language and similar customs emerged. Yet it was not until Germany colonized Tanzania that the remaining clans combined into one society. Today the Chagga are renowned for having a strong sense of identity and pride and are one of the richest and most powerful clans in Tanzania.

Kilimanjaro History Makers

The first large-scale attempt to summit Mount Kilimanjaro took place in August of 1861. Baron Carl Claus von der Decken, a Hanoverian naturalist, failed to reach the summit after two attempts. On his first attempt, von der Decken used a climbing party of over fifty porters and a manservant but had to turn back after three days because of poor weather conditions. During his first attempt the Baron witnessed and described the summit of Kibo as: "Bathed in a flood of rosy light, the cap that crowns the mountain's noble brow gleamed in the dazzling glory of the setting sun."

Von der Decken provided the most accurate estimate for the height of both Kibo—between 19,812 and 20,655 feet in elevation—and Mawenzi—between 17,257 and 17,453. The expeditions also led to the belief that the mountain was volcanic in origin, with Shira being the oldest cone and Kibo the newest. Although the Baron's first attempt only allowed him to reach approximately 8,000 feet, his second attempt reached 14,200. Unfortunately, again he was faced with insurmountable weather problems and, due to a snow storm, was forced to retreat from his quest.

The Uhuru Peak of Kilimanjaro's volcanic cone, Kibo, was summited in 1889 by Hans Meyer. Meyer made his first attempt to summit the mountain in 1887 and his second in 1888. On his third attempt, he finally conquered Kilimanjaro. The largest obstacle Meyer faced in his expeditions was a lack of sustenance as he climbed closer to the summit. He was not able to pack enough food to last throughout the expedition. To solve this, he established camps at various points along the route, and at the camps he stored food. Porters carried supplies up to the camps weekly, which allowed Meyer to make multiple summit attempts in one expedition without having to return to the base of Kilimanjaro to replenish his supplies.

After his summit, Meyer wrote of his adventures in his book, *Across East African Glaciers*. The book describes Meyer's efforts to carve stairs into an ice cliff. It is said that each stair needed an average of twenty blows from Meyer's ice axe. Three days later, on October 6th, 1889, Meyer crossed the Kibo crater and reached Uhuru, the highest point on Kilimanjaro.

Hans Meyer was accompanied by a considerable climbing entourage. The mountaineering party consisted of his climbing companion, Ludwig Purtscheller, two local headmen, nine porters, three other locals who acted as supervisors, one cook, and one guide. The guide was supplied by the local Chagga chief, Mareale, whom Meyer had befriended in his first expedition in 1887. The porters and supervisors were used to relay supplies to the camps.

Currently, the record of fastest summit, ascent and descent of Mount Kilimanjaro belongs to Simon Mtuy of Tanzania. Mtuy manages the Summit Expeditions and Nomadic Experience trekking agency in Moshi. His long experience at high-altitude climbing gave him the stamina to complete the climb, On December 26, 2004, in eight hours and twenty-seven minutes. His ascent spanned over six hours; at the summit, Mtuy rested for seven minutes, then made the descent in two hours and twenty minutes.

About the Authors

Charles G. Irion

Charles G. Irion is a publisher, author, adventurer, entrepreneur, and philanthropist. In the 1970s, Irion began his career in commercial real estate development and brokerage. In 1983, he founded U.S. Park Investments, a company that owns and brokers manufactured home and RV communities. Over the years, Irion has garnered a large collection of recipes from resident RV campers. More than 350 of these can be found in his book, *Roadkill Cooking for Campers: The Best Dang Wild Game Cookbook in the World.*

In 2007, Irion founded Irion Books LLC and began writing and publishing books. His first volume was *Remodeling Hell*—one of four books he authored as part of the Hell Series. This was followed by *Autograph Hell, Car Dealer Hell,* and *Divorce Hell.* Inspired by real-life events, these books are true stories created by actual (hellish) events that infuriated Irion to the point of wanting to expose the demons through his writings and to guide others on how to avoid the same 'Hell' he experienced. He is donating all of the net proceeds of his Hell Series to victims of fraud.

While writing the Hell Series, Irion began work on the Summit Murder Mystery series. The impetus behind the murder mystery series was his participation in a 1987 expedition to Mount Everest from the

China side. Irion couldn't resist creating plot-twisting, adventure-filled stories against the backdrop of the Seven Summits, the highest and deadest mountains on the world's seven continents. In June of 2011, Irion joined a climbing expedition to Kilimanjaro. The trip included a medical mission with the K2 Adventures Foundation, a non-profit organization and one of Irion's philanthropic endeavors.

He also supports other humanitarian-relief organizations, such as Project C.U.R.E. and Healing the Children. Recently he traveled to Belize and Cuba with Project C.U.R.E. on Philanthropic Travel missions.

Charles Irion holds a Masters of Business Administration in International Marketing and Finance from the American Graduate School of International Management, and Bachelor of Arts degrees in both Biology and Economics from the University of California, Santa Barbara.

As an explorer, Irion has visited more than 60 countries and is an accomplished SCUBA diver. He is also the founder of a children's dictionary charity, a founding member of Phoenix Social Venture Partners, is involved in Lions Club International, is a past treasurer of the Lions Club Sight & Hearing Foundation, and is currently an advisory board member of Project C.U.R.E. Irion lives in Arizona.

To learn more about Charles Irion, please visit: www.CharlesIrion.com

Ronald J. Watkins

Ronald J. Watkins is an American writer of novels and nonfiction. Watkins has also served as co-author, collaborator, or editor for more than thirty books. He is the founder and principal writer for Watkins & Associates. In 1993, Watkins published *Birthright,* the saga of the Shoen family, which founded and owned U-Haul International and of the then-unsolved murder of Eva Shoen. When he refused to identify his sources under subpoena, he was twice found in contempt by a federal court, with his position being upheld by the Ninth Circuit on both occasions.

These established case law sustaining the right of authors of nonfiction books to refuse to identify either confidential or non-confidential sources. For Watkins' defense of the First Amendment, he was recognized as a finalist for the PEN/Newman's Own First Amendment Award.

Watkins' first book, *High Crimes and Misdemeanors,* was an account of the impeachment of Arizona governor Evan Mecham. Written just one year after the events and based on hundreds of interviews with participants, it remains the definitive account of an American impeachment.

He then authored *Evil Intentions,* the story of the brutal murder of Suzanne Rossetti in Phoenix, Arizona. It was followed a few years later by *Against Her Will,* the story of the murder of Kelly Tinyes in Valley Stream, Long Island, New York. This was the first murder case in the State of New York solved in large part by DNA testing.

In 2003, John Murray (UK) published Watkins' book, *Unknown Seas: How Vasco da Gama Opened the East.* The following year, Watkins was nominated for the Mountbatten Maritime Prize in the United Kingdom. The book has since been published in Portuguese in Brazil and in Czech in the Czech Republic.

Watkins is co-author, with Charles G. Irion, of the Summit Murder Mysteries series, novels set on the highest mountains in the world. In all, the series is projected to include seven books, plus a prequel book titled *Abandoned on Everest.* He holds a Bachelor of Arts in History and a Master of Science in Justice Studies. Following university, he worked as a probation officer and presentencing investigator for the Superior Court in Phoenix, Arizona. He is a former chief administrative law judge and was assistant director of the Arizona Department of Insurance, where he served as Arizona's chief insurance fraud investigator.

Watkins has been called on by the media and has made a number of television and radio appearances, including Dominick Dunne's *Power, Privilege, and Justice; PrimeTime! with Tom Brokaw and Katie Couric; Under Scrutiny with Jane Wallace; Geraldo with Geraldo Rivera,* and *American Forum* national radio program.

To learn more about Ronald J. Watkins, please visit: www.RonaldjWatkins.com

Summit Murder Mystery Series

The Summit Murder Mystery Series explores murders set on the Seven Summits, the highest and deadliest mountains on the world's seven continents.

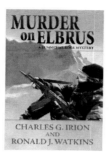
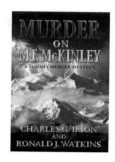

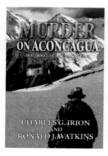

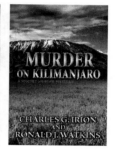

Murder on Everest
Murder on Elbrus
Murder on Mt. McKinley
Murder on Puncak Jaya
Murder on Aconcagua
Murder on Vinson Massif
Murder on Kilimanjaro

The Summit Murder Mystery Series is available in paperback and E-book for Kindle, Nook, Sony, iPad and other Eformats.

For audio versions visit SummitMurderMystery.com

www.Seven7Summits.com
www.IrionBooks.com
Facebook.com/IrionBooks
twitter.com/CharlesIrion

THE MAP OF MURDER

Summit Murder Mystery Series

SummitMurderMystery.com